# A CORNISH BETRAYAL

When Loveday inherits the ruins of a remote clifftop cottage, her delight is marred by the mysterious disappearance of a young man from his narrowboat on a Cornish creek. Since he's a chum of her friends, Keri and Ben, she naturally wants to help. But things quickly escalate into a far more serious affair, and it seems her involvement could be doing more harm than good. Despite Loveday's best intentions to steer clear of her detective boyfriend Sam's investigation, she becomes inextricably involved — risking her life in the process . . .

RENA GEORGE

# A CORNISH
# BETRAYAL

*Complete and Unabridged*

**LINFORD**
*Leicester*

First published in Great Britain

First Linford Edition
published 2018

A catalogue record for this book is available
from the British Library.

ISBN 978–1–4448–3562–5

Published by
F. A. Thorpe (Publishing)
Anstey, Leicestershire

Set by Words & Graphics Ltd.
Anstey, Leicestershire
Printed and bound in Great Britain by
T. J. International Ltd., Padstow, Cornwall

This book is printed on acid-free paper

# 1

Keri gave her friend a curious frown. 'You have a strange faraway look tonight, Loveday. Care to share anything with us?'

Loveday glanced away from the pinks and golds of the sunset she could see from the tiny cottage window, and turned to the three others around the table.

'Sorry, I'm not great company tonight.' She gave Keri and Ben an apologetic grin. 'And after your magnificent spag bol too. You must give Sam your recipe.'

'Ignore her, she's being facetious,' Sam said, putting his hand over the top of his wine glass to turn down Ben's offer of a top up. 'Loveday knows that my culinary skills are strictly limited to collecting the takeaways.'

Keri gave him a puzzled stare, but Loveday cut in. 'He's not joking. Sam's not exactly a cordon bleu chef, but then neither am I.'

Keri tilted her head and looked from

one to the other. 'You don't look as if you're exactly fading away from malnutrition.'

Loveday smiled. 'That's because we dine out at the Godolphin so much. Sam likes to keep me in the style I've grown accustomed to.'

'Becoming a property owner is changing you already,' he laughed.

'Property owner?' Keri's head snapped up. 'You kept that a big secret. Well come on, don't keep us in the dark. Have you come into a fortune?'

'Not exactly,' Loveday said. 'In fact not at all. It's more like a pile of rubble that's been left to me by an ancient aunt I've never even met.'

As she spoke, Loveday's mind flicked back to the surprise phone call from her mother.

'I have some bad news for you,' Heather Ross had said.

Loveday's heart had thudded. 'It's not Dad, is it? Has something happened?'

'No, of course not,' Heather had cut in quickly. 'It's your great-aunt Martha. I've had a call from her grandson, Peter. I'm afraid she's passed away.'

Loveday frowned, trying to remember great-aunt Martha, but she'd searched her memory in vain. The woman sounded like a character from a Dickens novel.

'You probably don't remember her,' Heather had said. 'They emigrated to Canada before you were born. Granddad was the one who kept in touch with them.'

Loveday's grandfather, Marack Yelland, was in his eighties now, and quite frail. Convincing him to leave his beloved Cornwall when her grandmother, Rose, died three years earlier had not been easy, but her parents had eventually persuaded him to move into the little bungalow next to the family pub in the Black Isle near Inverness. He was settled there now, and she knew her mother was happier having him close by.

'Believe it or not, your brother, Hugh, taught him to use the Internet, so he has been keeping in touch with Peter through emails.'

Loveday smiled. Her granddad had been emailing her too. They were

3

touching little notes full of sad, thoughtful memories of the old days and his life in Cornwall with her lovely and much missed grannie.

'Anyway, as I said, Peter rang last night,' her mother had continued. 'But it was late so I thought it best to put off calling you until now.'

Loveday felt a pang of regret. She should have made more of an effort to visit Peter and the rest of the family in Canada.

She'd said, 'I'm so sorry, Mum. Are you OK?'

'I'm fine but Granddad was quite emotional when I told him this morning. He's been relieving the old days and the family history back when his father, Edward Yelland, and sisters, Alice and Martha were brought up in Carn Hendra.'

'Carn Hendra?'

'It was a tiny stone cottage down in the wilds of West Cornwall.'

'It sounds like a hard life,' Loveday had said.

'It certainly would have been for

Martha and her husband, Henry, back in those days. He was a tin miner. Their daughter, Christa — Peter's mother — was married to another miner, and she was a bal maiden.'

Loveday had heard about the tough lives of the bal maidens. They were employed to break the ore for smelting. She was trying to imagine the women using their heavy hammers to smash the stone into small pieces. She shook her head, such exhausting, dirty work, and all for a pittance in pay.

'When's the funeral?' she'd asked.

'It's already taken place two days ago in Ontario,' Heather had told her. 'But there's more. Apparently Aunt Martha still owned the family property in Cornwall.' She'd taken a breath. 'The thing is, Loveday. She's left it to you.'

Loveday had gasped. 'She's left me a house?'

'Not a house exactly, it's a cottage . . . well, what's left of it, although I expect it must be pretty much a ruin by now. It's years since I was out there but I can vaguely picture it. I didn't know it was still in the family. No one has lived there for years.'

Loveday's mind switched back to the present and she realized that everyone was looking at her.

'Well, don't leave it there, Loveday. Tell us about it.' Keri's look of excitement made Loveday smile.

'I haven't come into a fortune,' she said quickly, explaining about her mother's surprise telephone call, and her own amazement at the gift from her elderly great-aunt.

'It's a rundown cottage over Zennor way,' she said. 'It might not even still be standing. Probably only a scattering of stones by now.'

Keri raised an eyebrow. 'You mean you haven't been to see it yet?'

'Not yet, I've only now heard about it.'

'What will you do with it?' Ben asked.

Loveday grimaced. 'Absolutely no idea. I'm going over there tomorrow to have a look.' She glanced at Sam. 'Fancy coming with me?'

'Not sure,' Sam said. 'Depends on what I have on tomorrow, but things are quiet at the moment so it should be fine.'

Keri had slipped into the kitchen and reappeared with a big red coffee pot and four mugs on a tray. She nodded back to the kitchen and Ben went to collect the cheese board.

Loveday sat back surveying the array of cheeses and savoury biscuits and gave her tummy a pat. 'Not sure I've got room for any more food.'

'I'm sure you can manage something,' Keri said, but her attention was on Ben, and when Loveday followed her gaze she caught the worried frown. And now that she thought about it, he had been very quiet during the meal.

'Everything all right, Ben?' she asked.

'What?' He glanced across at her. 'Yes, everything's fine.' But he hadn't been able to disguise his distracted look. Sam had noticed it, too.

'You might as well tell them,' Keri said.

'Tell us what?' Sam's head had come up.

Ben swallowed and Loveday saw the muscles in his jaw working.

'Go on,' Keri encouraged.

He sighed. 'One of my friends has disappeared.'

They all stared at him.

'It's probably nothing but . . . well, I'm getting worried.'

'Disappeared? What do you mean disappeared?' Sam's expression was serious. In the three years he'd known Ben he could never have described him as fanciful. In fact for an artist, he was remarkably down to earth. So what was this about?

'You mean your friend has gone off somewhere?' Loveday interrupted.

'That's just it. I have no idea. He was going to show me round his boat. Jamie has been living on an old narrowboat he's renovating down near Karrek. But when I turned up on Monday he was nowhere to be seen. And he hadn't slept on the boat the previous night.'

'Who told you that?' Sam asked.

'Scobey, the old boy who's been helping him with the boat. He didn't look very happy about the situation either. He said it wasn't like Jamie to go away and not mention it.'

'And this was five days ago?' Sam said. Ben nodded.

'How do you know he hasn't come back?' Loveday asked.

'He hadn't come back yesterday. I checked. As I said, I'm starting to worry.'

'Starting?' Keri repeated. 'You've been worrying about this all week.' She turned to Sam. 'Something's not right, Sam. We are both beginning to think this is serious.'

Loveday had been studying Keri's face. Her friend was her PA at *Cornish Folk*, the Truro-based magazine she edited. And if Keri felt this Jamie's sudden disappearance warranted concern then they should listen.

Sam was also feeling uncomfortable about Ben's story, but he tried to keep his tone light. 'Does Jamie have a girlfriend?'

'I think so,' Ben said. 'He's mentioned a girl called Maya, but I've no idea who she is, or where she lives.' His shoulders lifted in a helpless shrug. 'Scobey's right. It's not like Jamie to just disappear. He would have told someone what he was doing.' He would have told Scobey or left a message for me explaining he'd had to go away.'

'Not if he didn't want anyone to know where he was,' Keri said. 'You told me he didn't get on with his parents. Maybe they've been trying to find him and he's lying low for a while.'

'Why would he do that?' Loveday chimed in. She was thinking of her own family and how close they all were. It was inconceivable to her not to get on with your parents. Whenever any of her family came to visit her in Cornwall it was cause for celebration.

'Jamie's folks are Sarah and Charles Roscow.'

It was clear Ben expected her and Sam to recognize the names, but they didn't. Loveday pressed her lips together and shrugged.

'The father runs some big London investment bank,' Ben continued. 'Jamie's mother is involved in it too. They live in a sumptuous pad somewhere behind Harrods.

'They wanted Jamie to join them in the business but he had other ideas, which is why he came to Cornwall. As far as I know his parents have disowned him.' He frowned. 'I think he got involved with some undesirables in London. He wasn't exactly doing drugs, but I think he might have dabbled.'

'But they must know he's down here,' Loveday said.

Ben shook his head. 'I doubt it. Jamie went to great lengths to make sure they didn't find him — hence the boat.'

Sam had stayed silent over the last minutes. He was thinking. The lad had only been missing — if he actually *was* missing — for five days. He could reel off any number of legitimate reasons why he'd gone away, but something was beginning to bug him and he didn't like the troubled feeling that was beginning to settle in the pit of his stomach. He hoped he was wrong.

'I take it you haven't reported Jamie missing yet, Ben?'

'No, I wanted to run it past you and Loveday first.'

'Well, as you say, it's only been five days, and there could be plenty of explanations for that. But you're obviously concerned . . . '

'You see! What have I been saying, Ben?' Keri interrupted. 'Sam agrees with me. You should report it to the police. Tomorrow is Saturday. I'm not working. We can go into Truro together.'

'Someone else might have already done it . . . maybe Scobey. I don't want to waste anyone's time.'

'You wouldn't be doing that,' Sam reassured him.

'I don't suppose you could make a few enquiries, Sam, before it all gets official? You said things were quiet with you at the moment.'

'I can maybe put out a few feelers, but I'm not promising anything. There's not much the police can do unless you file a missing person report.'

'I can't see there would be any harm in it,' Loveday agreed.

Ben was still looking unsure, but Keri thumped the table as she stood up to clear away the coffee things. 'That's settled then. We'll go to the police in the morning.'

'Sounds like a plan, Ben.' Sam gave what he hoped was an encouraging smile.

'You think I should?'

'Definitely!' Loveday said.

# 2

'What did you really make of Ben's story about his missing friend?' Loveday slid Sam a glance as they drove in his old silver Lexus towards Zennor next morning. 'It does sound a bit funny, don't you think?'

He did. In fact the more he thought about it the more uncomfortable he felt, but he wasn't about to share his fears with Loveday. It wasn't as if she could do anything about it, but he had no doubt she might try.

'I think we shouldn't be making a fuss. Jamie could turn up any time,' he said.

'But you told Ben to report him missing. We all did.'

'And I'd do it again,' Sam said. 'If only to put his mind at rest that he'd done all he could.'

'So you don't think anything's happened to this Jamie?'

Sam frowned. 'Like what?' He really

ought to shut down this conversation, but he couldn't lie to Loveday. He sighed. 'Look, I've no more idea than anyone else about the whereabouts of this lad, and no reason to suppose anything's happened to him, but if Ben reports him missing then we'll check it out.'

They had turned off the road and were following a rough track that wound its way through wild rock-strewn pasture. As they came over a ridge they both gasped at the wide expanse of ocean that had come into view. Sam brought the car to a halt and for a moment neither of them spoke as they took in the vista of sea and sky.

'It's so beautiful!' Loveday said.

Sam nodded, he wasn't given to waxing lyrical about the scenery. Cornwall had many quaint villages, turquoise seas and picturesque coves, but the raw wildness of what he was now seeing brought a lump to even his throat. He swallowed it back and said, 'Well, we know where the sea is, so where is your cottage?'

Loveday twisted round to stare out across the bracken moors. She had no idea where her great-aunt Martha's property was. She reached down and fished the Ordnance Survey map from under the passenger seat and spread it out on her knee, tracing a finger along the coast.

Sam gave her a dubious grin. 'I'm not sure a map will be much help if this place really is a pile of stones.'

'It's called Carn Hendra. It might be here. I could have missed it last time I looked.' But Loveday knew she hadn't missed it. Carn Hendra was not on any map. She looked up again, squinting into the distance. 'We're not going to find it, are we?'

Sam put an arm around her shoulders and gave her a squeeze. 'Come on. We're here now so let's get out and have a look around.'

Loveday bit her lip, still squinting about her. She was trying to remember what her mother had told her about the place. She repeated the description Martha's grandson had given. He'd said Carn Hendra had the sea on its right and the rising moors to the left. She gave a dejected sigh. That description could apply to anywhere around here.

They spent a fruitless hour wandering the clifftop. The wind had got up, bending the tips of the bracken. Out to sea it looked like a storm was rolling in. Somewhere in the distance Loveday detected the sound of an engine. She listened. 'I can hear something.'

Sam frowned into the breeze. Yes, he'd heard it too — and then he smiled. 'It's a tractor.'

They both turned from the sea, sweeping their gaze over the rough terrain. 'There!' Sam pointed. 'There it is. Way over on the far side of that field.'

Loveday could see it now, and her heart gave an excited little flip. 'Are you thinking what I'm thinking?'

They were already starting towards the tractor.

'Now don't get your hopes up, Loveday,' Sam warned. 'This driver might be a young lad who doesn't even know this area.'

Loveday threw him a scowl and Sam put up his hands in a gesture of mock defence. 'I'm only saying.' He laughed. 'But since we've come this far I suppose anything's worth a try.'

Loveday had picked up her pace and was now striding out ahead of him. As they got closer they could see that the tractor was red. The driver spotted them heading towards him and stopped the vehicle.

'Hey there,' he called out. 'What are you doing on my land?'

He wasn't a young man at all. Loveday's spirits rose. The weather-beaten face creased into an irritated stare.

'We're sorry to interrupt your work,' Loveday called up to him. 'We're looking for a cottage called Carn Hendra. Can you help us?'

The old man killed the engine, took off his woolly hat and scratched a mop of grey hair. He glared suspiciously at them. 'Carn Hendra, you say?'

Loveday nodded and waited.

'You're mistaken. There is no Carn Hendra.' He reached out to restart the tractor.

'Is there someone else we can ask?'

Loveday shouted over the noisy engine.

'Nobody,' he wheezed. 'There is no Carn Hendra. I told you.' He drew his bushy white eyebrows together and stared down at her. 'What's your interest, anyhow?'

'I thought you said there was no such place?' Sam interrupted.

The old man nodded out across the rough fields. 'Not now there ain't — not no more.'

Loveday and Sam looked at each other. The man seemed to be considering whether to take this conversation any further, and then he lifted his arm and pointed. 'Can you see the field o'er yonder?'

Loveday and Sam peered into the distance.

Loveday shrugged. All she could see was rough stony ground. 'There's nothing there,' she said.

The old farmer gave an exasperated sigh. 'Isn't that what I've been telling you. There is no Carn Hendra.' He paused. 'But that's where it used to be. It's only a heap of rubbish now.'

He gave them a suspicious glance. 'Why would you be wanting to know?'

Loveday told her story, and stepped back as the farmer reached to switch off his engine, eased himself out of the tight seat, and clambered down, puffing breathlessly.

'The name's Clem Tangye,' he said, making no effort to offer them his hand. 'You'll be my new neighbours then?'

Loveday tilted her head at him and narrowed her eyes. 'I thought you said there was nothing left of the cottage?'

'I said it was a heap of rubbish, but the land's still there. If you own Carn Hendra cottage then the land belongs to you as well.' He fixed Sam with a questioning stare. 'Reckon that's right, don't you?'

Sam nodded. 'That would be my thinking.'

Loveday had never considered there would be any land with the cottage, but of course, there must have been. In the past, when her ancestors would have resided in the dwelling, they would have lived off the land. She was beginning to feel quite excited.

'If you're planning to have a look over there.' The man nodded towards the wild field. 'I'll come with you.'

Loveday and Sam suppressed a grin.

'That would be very kind of you Mr Tangye.'

'Clem,' he corrected.

'All right.' Loveday laughed. 'Clem.'

Her anticipation mounted, as they got closer to the field. She could see it was strewn with rocks and stones, and right in the middle was a more concentrated area of boulders.

'That's it,' Clem said. 'That's your cottage.'

The sky had darkened and a fierce wind was blowing sheets of rain straight off the sea. It felt like Loveday's ancestors were scolding her for not having visited them sooner. A shiver ran down her spine and she reached for Sam's hand.

They could hear the waves crashing at the bottom of the cliffs. Even in this weather the place had a remote raw beauty. Loveday closed her eyes, trying to imagine what it would have been like for her great-aunt Martha's family, battered by winter storms, and scratching a living from this land.

She had seen sketches of these little cottages — four low walls of granite boulders, and roof timbers probably dragged from the beach following a shipwreck. The structure would have been topped with sods of earth or a thatch of heather and straw.

A surge of sadness swept through her as she stared at the tumble of boulders. This little cottage might have provided shelter, but there would have been very little comfort. Her family must have suffered such hardship here.

Suddenly she understood Martha's bequest. She had wanted her to stand on this spot and feel what she was feeling now. It was a link to her past.

She blinked back a prick of tears. 'This is the source, Sam,' she whispered, her voice shaking. 'This is where my family belonged.'

Sam reached out to stroke Loveday's wet hair and planted a kiss on top of her head.

The old farmer looked away, embarrassed by the tender gesture. 'The pair of you's getting soaked,' he muttered gruffly, 'and I have to be moving on. You should be getting back to you's car.'

'What's that?' Sam said, pointing to what looked like the entrance to a cave in the side of the hill just ahead of them.

'You don't want to be going there.' Clem wheezed. 'Nobody goes there.'

'They might if they were getting soaked,' Sam retorted. 'Our car's half an hour away. It looks like we can shelter over there until this blows over. I don't suppose you have a torch?'

The old man frowned. 'Why would I be having a torch? Stay away from that place. I told you.'

'If we're going to be neighbours Mr . . . er, Clem. We should at least know where you live,' Loveday said. To her surprise, he pointed. 'We're over there at the back of the hill, but we don't encourage no visitors.'

Loveday smiled. Clem Tangye could hardly be described as the friendliest of individuals, but then she wasn't planning a restoration project for Carn Hendra cottage. She switched her attention back to the gap in the hill. 'Is it a cave?' she asked.

'It's a fogou if you're interested, and it's been there for more'n two thousand years, but it's not a place to visit.'

Loveday saw the old man shiver.

'Fogou?' she repeated. 'What's a fogou?'

Sam pulled up the collar of his jacket, anxious to be off.

Clem Tangye ignored the driving rain, his stare on the opening in the hillside. 'It's old, and dark, and creepy, and that's all you need to know.'

'Does it belong to me?' Loveday persisted. 'It's on Carn Hendra land.'

'Can we debate the ownership later,' Sam said, grabbing Loveday's arm, and bringing their conversation with the farmer to an end as he hurried them to the shelter of the fogou.

The old man stood looking after them for a moment, the rain streaming down his face. He knew it would happen one day. Somebody was bound to come looking for the place. Soon his secret would be out, and there was nothing he could do about it. His head was down and his shoulders slumped as he slowly walked back to his tractor.

# 3

Sam and Loveday tore across the rain-lashed field and ducked, laughing and breathless, into the low entrance of the fogou. Still laughing they brushed the droplets of rain off each other's jackets and stared out at the passing storm.

'It won't last,' Sam said, keeping his eye on the weather.

'Shame.' Loveday gave him a mischievous grin. 'I was beginning to enjoy it.'

'Only mad people love the rain. You know that, don't you?'

She gave him a playful slap. 'Don't be such a wimp. It's only water.'

'Well, right now it's trickling down the back of my neck. I'm not loving it.'

Loveday had glanced around and was peering into the dark space behind them. Even here at the entrance to the cave the air smelled musty.

'We could have done with that torch.' She was already venturing into the tunnel

26

when Sam got out his mobile phone and switched on the torch app.

He touched her arm. 'You stay here. Remember what that farmer said.'

'No way,' Loveday insisted. 'I'm not staying back here on my own while you have all the fun. I'm coming with you.'

Sam swung the torch beam in her face and shook his head, grinning. 'Well, don't go wandering off on your own. Stay close to me.'

Loveday quite liked the way Sam was protective of her, but she wasn't about to tell him that. So she gave him a little push and told him to stop fussing.

The earthy damp smell intensified and filled their nostrils as they crept slowly on, being careful not to stumble on the rough stone floor. The beam of the torch made the long dark passage ahead seem endless.

'How far do you think this goes?' Loveday's voice came out in a reverent whisper.

'Hang on,' Sam said, 'I think I can see daylight ahead.' He flicked the torch off. Loveday moved closer, clutching his back as they were plunged into darkness. The place had a strange atmosphere — and she wasn't sure she liked it.

But as her eyes grew used to the darkness she saw what Sam meant. It did look as though daylight was seeping into the passage further ahead.

'You OK, Loveday? Do you want to go back?'

'No. Let's push on. Maybe there's a way out along there.' She nodded towards the dim light.

Sam flicked the torch back on as they closed the distance to the shaft of light. The passage opened into a small, approximately 10ft × 10ft chamber. There was a rusty iron grid above them, through which the rain was pouring in.

Loveday scanned the walls of the chamber and then paused. 'Look,' she said. 'There's another passage!'

The fact that she could now see daylight again had fired her with more confidence. She tugged at Sam's arm. 'We can't not look,' she urged.

Sam wasn't sharing Loveday's excitement. Something wasn't right — and it wasn't just the darkness.

'You stay here,' he instructed. 'Let me have a quick scout around and then I'll come back for you.'

Loveday stared at him. 'Of course I'm coming with you.'

Sam suppressed a sigh. There was no point in telling Loveday what to do.

'Well, come then.' He said.

She made a little shooing gesture and said, 'Let's go.'

With a growing feeling of unrest, Sam led the way. They were about twenty yards into the passage when the sickly smell hit him, almost making him gag. His arm shot out, stopping Loveday moving any further forward.

She had a hand over her mouth and nose. 'What's that awful stench?'

'OK, we're going back. At least you are.' This time he wasn't taking no for an answer.

Loveday took a quick side step and her foot hit something, throwing her off balance. She let out a little yell as she threw out a hand for the stone wall to steady her. The object at her foot hadn't felt like a stone. Even before Sam shone the torch in her direction she knew what had caused her stumble.

She fought back a surge of nausea. She couldn't throw up down here . . . not in this place. Sam had put an arm around her. 'Come on,' he said urgently. 'Let's get you out of here.'

She was trembling uncontrollably and her legs felt so wobbly she didn't think they would hold her.

'You'll be fine, love. It's the shock.'

'It's the smell,' Loveday said. Even her voice was shaking. 'That awful smell.'

'I know,' Sam said. 'Try not to think about it.' He was already on his mobile, punching in his detective sergeant, Will Tregellis's, number. It was a reflex action because there was no way he would have a signal down here in the tunnel. But when they reached the chamber, to his surprise, his mobile sprung into life.

He hit the button again. It was answered in a split second.

Sam's voice was icy cold. 'Will? It's me,' he said sharply. 'We've got a body.'

Loveday slumped against the side of

30

the chamber, trying to stay calm as Sam gave their location and instructed Will what to do.

She was grateful for Sam's strong arm around her as they made their way to the entrance to the fogou. The rain had stopped and Loveday held up her face to the grey sky, gulping in the sharp, sea air. Another time the afternoon would have seemed gloomy, but following the horror of what she'd seen back in the fogou, the dark clouds were like the best sight in the world.

'You've had a shock,' Sam said, sliding an arm around her again and pulling her close. 'You shouldn't have seen that. It's all my fault. I should have stopped you going into that passage.'

'Of course it wasn't your fault, Sam.' She pulled back to look up into his face and her heart contracted at the concern she saw there. 'It was me who insisted on following you in.' She pushed a hand through her long dark hair, tucking it behind her ears. 'I don't know why I reacted like that. It's not as though I haven't seen a dead body before.'

31

'You shouldn't be seeing any dead bodies. That's my job.'

Loveday knew what he meant, but things didn't always work out the way they should, and right now she was getting flashbacks of terrible images from the past.

In her mind's eye it was a few years ago, and she was back on the cliffs at Borlase with her artist friend, Lawrence Kemp, taking pictures for the magazine feature she was planning to do about his work. It was his dog, Flossie, that had alerted them to the body far below in the cove.

Loveday swallowed back the rising dread. She didn't want to relive that awful moment again, but the sickening image kept flashing into her head. Once again she was on the edge of the cliff, staring down into the cove. She could see it quite clearly . . . the body emerging from the receding tide. It had been staked into the shingle. There was no way of escape. She tried not to imagine the poor man's terror as the waves crept up his body and over his face. She shuddered. Other memories were pounding in . . .

There was poor Jago Tilley in Marazion, but that didn't count because it was her friend, Priddy Rodda, who had found her old neighbour lying in a pool of blood at the foot of his stairs. Loveday had been in her landlady Cassie's kitchen the day Priddy rushed in looking for Cassie's GP husband, Adam. The old lady was so distressed that Adam had asked Loveday to go back to Jago's cottage with them. So she had seen the body — and it wasn't a nice memory.

'You're white as a ghost, Loveday.' Sam's worried voice brought her back to the present. He touched her cheek. 'We have to get you away from here.'

'Actually, I'm feeling much better,' she lied. 'Don't worry about me. You've got enough on your plate.' She glanced back to the fogou. 'How long do you think he's been in there?'

'We don't yet know that it is a *he*, Bartholomew will be able to tell us more when he arrives.'

Dr Robert Bartholomew, Home Office pathologist, was a gruff big-bearded man who wasted no time on niceties. Loveday knew he wasn't going to enjoy being called to this place.

Detective Constable Amanda Fox was the first of Sam's team to arrive on the scene. She came squelching over the rough terrain in her green wellies, and gave Loveday a brief nod before following Sam to the entrance of the fogou. 'I was in Penzance on that burglary enquiry,' she heard her explain. 'Will told me to drop everything and just get here. He's mobilized the whole works so they're all on the way. What have we got, boss?'

'A body. It's quite a way in. I want to wait for the Scenes of Crime team before we wade in again,' Sam said.

The DC threw another glance in Loveday's direction. 'So . . . what?' She wrinkled her brow. 'You were just in there exploring, and came upon a body?' Clearly she thought they were mad.

'That's about it, DC Fox,' Sam said icily. 'Now tell me where you've parked because my car is miles away.'

'About fifty yards over there.' She pointed. 'There's a rough track. It's not the best terrain, but the troops should manage.' She was staring at the entrance to the passage. 'Is this the only way into the . . . ' She paused. 'Well, what is this place exactly? Is it a cave?'

'It's a fogou,' Loveday said. 'It could have been here for two thousand years.'

Amanda's expression suggested she wasn't impressed.

Sam sighed. He wanted the rest of his team down here — and fast. 'We don't know if this is the only way in,' he said. 'There's a chamber about thirty yards or so along with a kind of metal grid to the outside in the roof.' Sam looked down at Amanda's boots. 'You could make yourself useful by trying to locate it on the surface.' He pointed across the sodden field. 'It should be somewhere over there.'

The DC frowned. It wasn't a task she relished. She wanted to be in with the body — like a real murder detective.

'Don't worry, Constable, we'll send out a search party if we haven't heard back from you by dark,' Sam said, not allowing any amusement at Amanda's obvious annoyance, to creep into his voice. 'But don't take that long, we might need to use that chamber as a way in. I doubt if SOCO will want our lot's great boots tramping over any evidence around the main passage.'

Amanda managed a grim nod, making a mental note never to arrive first at a potential crime scene again. The early birds always got the crap jobs.

The cavalcade of police vehicles began arriving ten minutes later. Detective Sergeant Will Tregellis was first out. Loveday watched Sam striding towards him. He was in policeman mode now. He'd forgotten all about her.

# 4

An hour earlier the wild desolate clifftop had felt like a remote and secluded place, but now it was teeming with people. The well-rehearsed machine that was the police crime-investigating unit was at full tilt.

Scenes of Crime officers in their white boiler suits had set up a stepping stones arrangement of plastic squares, creating a path into the fogou that reduced contamination to a minimum.

In the distance Loveday could see Amanda waving to her colleagues, indicating that she had located the big metal grill to the underground chamber. Soon large spotlights were being carried across the field to it.

Over by the entrance to the fogou, Sam and Will were deep in conversation. No one had noticed Loveday wandering off, and now she watched them all as she sat on a large boulder on the site of Carn

Hendra — her inheritance.

A few hours ago she had been excited at the prospect of seeing the site but now she wondered if she would ever be able to remember it in a happy way again. It would always be the place where she and Sam found the body.

She'd been so deep in thought that she hadn't noticed Sam approaching, and the sound of his voice startled her.

'You OK, Loveday?' He tilted his head and gave her that concerned stare that always made her heart flip over.

She sighed. 'I'm trying to stay out of everyone's way.'

'Come here,' he said, holding out his arms to her. 'This isn't the day we had planned, is it?'

She moved closer to him, but not close enough to embrace. Such a show of affection by the senior officer at a crime scene was bound to cause talk. She nodded across to what looked like organized activity.

'Is it a murder, Sam?'

The big detective nodded grimly. 'Looks that way. Dr Bartholomew never says much, but there are head injuries.'

She nodded, still watching the busy scene with sad eyes. 'Poor man.'

For a few moments neither of them spoke, feeling the wind as it whipped around them, bending the bracken.

And then Sam said, 'I've told Amanda to take you home. There's no point in you hanging around here.'

When they arrived in Marazion, dark threatening clouds hung over the bay, and a clingy mist was totally obscuring the upper casement of St Michael's Mount. The causeway to the castle had disappeared under the high tide, making the mount an island once more.

The detective slowed the car as they approached the top of the drive to the big house where Cassie and Dr Adam Trevillick lived with their children, Sophie and Leo. Loveday's small cottage was right beside it.

'Thanks, Amanda. I appreciate the ride.'

The detective shrugged. 'No need for thanks. It wasn't my idea to give you a lift.'

Loveday shook her head as she watched

the car take off at speed along the front. She would have to resign herself to the fact that she and DC Amanda Fox would never be great friends!

She was about to let herself into her cottage when the kitchen door of the big house opposite was opened and Cassie appeared, looking distinctly worried.

'OK, what's happened . . . where's Sam? Please don't tell me you've had an accident?'

'Nothing's happened.' Loveday tried a reassuring smile. 'At least, we didn't have an accident.'

'So why did that young detective woman bring you home?' Cassie's expression softened. 'You look awful. I've got the kettle on next door, and Adam has taken the monsters to the cinema in Truro, so we can have a good old natter.'

Loveday wanted to curl up in her chair by the fire and shut out the gloom of this horrible day, but there was no point in refusing her friend's hospitality. Cassie wouldn't be satisfied until she'd got the whole story.

'Are you sure you only want tea? You

look like you need something stronger,' Cassie said as Loveday sat down at the big scrubbed kitchen table.

'Tea's fine.' She smiled, stretching back watching Cassie drop teabags into the pot, take milk from the fridge and unhook a couple of mugs from the shelf.

'Right . . . spill the beans,' Cassie said. 'Going to check out your new cottage obviously didn't go well.'

Loveday pushed a hand through her hair. She should have tied it up this morning. She could only imagine what a mess she must look.

Cassie fixed her with a stare. 'In your own time.'

Despite herself, Loveday relaxed. Renting her little cottage from Cassie and Adam was the best thing she had ever done. She couldn't have wished for better friends. She was 'auntie' to Sophie and Leo, and had been accepted as part of their family.

'The cottage is a pile of rubble,' Loveday said flatly.

Cassie's face crumpled into an expression of sympathy.

'I'm sorry, Loveday. I know how excited you were about it. You must be so disappointed.'

'A little.' Loveday sighed. 'But that's not what's upset me.' She paused before looking up and meeting Cassie's eyes.

'We found a body, Cassie.'

'What?' Her friend stared at her. 'What d'you mean found a body?'

'In this fogou thing on my land — at least the field that goes with the cottage.'

She explained how she and Sam had sheltered from the rain in the underground passage, and how events had escalated from there.

'You poor thing. That must have been horrible.' Cassie topped up Loveday's tea. 'So this skeleton was there in the passage.'

Loveday shook her head. 'No. It wasn't a skeleton. It was a man; at least I think it was a man. I almost tripped over him.'

Cassie clapped her hands to her cheeks. 'God, Loveday, trouble does seem to find you. Does Sam think this man was murdered?'

'He hasn't explicitly said so, but he's

pulled in all the troops and they've got the place sealed off like a crime scene.'

∗　∗　∗

Even as Sam rattled the heavy horseshoe knocker he knew there was no need because he'd seen the curtains move. He and Will were already being watched from the old farmhouse window. The face he'd seen quickly disappeared when its owner realized he had been spotted.

Sam waited. He was about to rattle the knocker again when the weather-ravaged door slowly opened and Farmer Tangye peered out at them.

'We need a few words with you, Mr Tangye,' Sam said.

The old man glanced over Sam's shoulder. 'What's going on? What are all that lot doing tramping all over my field? Nobody asked me for any permission to go messing about on my property.'

Sam turned and followed his gaze. The area was buzzing with police activity. He frowned. He wasn't in the mood for pointing out that the man had already told Loveday that the piece of land in question belonged to her.

'This is Detective Sergeant Tregellis, and I am Detective Inspector Kitto. May we come in, Mr Tangye?'

The farmer stepped aside with a grunt, and they followed him into a big, low-ceilinged front room. A log-burning stove glowed red in the fire recess, giving a cheerful welcome in contrast to the damp bleakness of the day outside.

A plump, grey-haired woman eyed them with suspicion from her chair by the fire.

'These be the police,' Clem Tangye said. 'This is my Lizzie.'

The woman gave the officers the briefest of nods before shooing a tiger-striped cat off her lap and struggling out of the chair.

'I suppose you'll be wanting some tea then?' She was already on her way to fill a kettle.

'That would be very welcome, Mrs Tangye.' Sam smiled. From the look on Will's face, he'd thought so too.

Sam waited until the tea had been

44

poured before asking, 'When was the last time you were in the fogou, Mr Tangye?' Sam deliberately kept his tone light . . . conversational, but the question still riled the old man.

'Only my enemies call me Mr Tangye,' he snapped. 'I told you before, you and the lass. The name's Clem.'

Sam nodded. 'Fine. So when was the last time you were in the fogou, Clem?'

'Never,' he barked. 'Why would I go down there? It's a horrible place. I told you before, didn't I? I told you not to go there. No good would come of it. I told you.'

'What exactly did you mean by that? If you've never been inside the place, why would you say it's horrible?'

'Ask anybody around these parts. You don't have to go into a graveyard at night to know it be an evil place. You just knows.'

Will raised an eyebrow and looked away. Either this man was the most superstitious he'd ever met, or he was nuts. He decided he was probably the latter.

'So nobody ever goes down there,' Sam persisted. 'Is that what you're saying?'

'No, that's not what I'm saying. You and the lass went down there, even when I warned you not to. The other pair went down an all.' He sighed. 'Nobody ever learns.'

'Other pair? What other pair?' Both detectives were staring at him.

'I don't know who they were, do I? I don't ask no questions. I just warn folks to stay away.' He got up and crossed to the window, frowning out at the police activity he could see in the distance. 'Not my fault if they pays no attention.'

Will couldn't contain his rising interest. 'So you say these people went into the fogou?'

Clem Tangye nodded.

Sam and Will exchanged a look.

'When was this Mr . . . emm, Clem?' Will asked.

'Three weeks ago,' Lizzie interrupted. 'You'd come back from ploughing that top field, Clem, and were wanting your supper when they came knocking.' She gave the faintest hint of a smile. 'Young

46

chap and his lass. They could just have gone out there — it's not as if there's any locks on the place — but they came and asked.' She looked across at her husband. 'It was definitely the day of the ploughing. It's in the calendar when you did that ploughing.'

'Aye I believe it was,' Clem said.

Sam pursed his lips, thinking. He wouldn't allow himself to get too excited about this new information. If Mrs Tangye's recollection of the date was accurate — and he believed it was — the young man couldn't be their body. According to the pathologist, the body was fresh — a few days at the most.

It was unlikely that this couple was connected to their body in the fogou, but if they had been inside the place it might give them a start. They'd have to find them first, of course.

'They definitely went into the fogou?' Will asked.

'They did,' said Mrs Tangye. 'I didn't see them going in of course, but I know they did because they came back and thanked us.'

'So you would recognize them again?' Will asked hopefully.

The woman nodded. 'I think so.'

'Did they mention why they wanted to see inside the fogou?' Sam asked.

'Only that they were interested in old things, standing stones and the like. They're all over Cornwall,' the woman replied.

Sam was warming to this woman. From her initial expression when they walked in he'd got the impression that he and Will would only be tolerated in this couple's home. Clem Tangye was not especially forthcoming, but his wife was definitely entitled to a gold star in Sam's book.

'I don't suppose they happened to mention where they were from?' Sam asked.

'Sorry.' Lizzie Tangye shook her head. 'The lad didn't say much at all, only that he lived on an old boat that he was renovating.' She put up a hand. 'And before you ask, the answer's no. I don't have any idea where his boat is. He never said.'

The little flicker of suspicion that had sparked deep inside Sam's head was now being fanned into a flame. He tried to keep his fears at bay. How many young men in Cornwall were living on old boats that they were renovating? Dozens? Hundreds? Sam knew of only one — and that's where their investigations would start. They would find Jamie Roscow.

# 5

'Of course I'm going with you,' Loveday said. 'Ben and Keri are my friends too.'

'It's not about that, Loveday. This is a police enquiry now. You have to leave it to me.'

'What if I promise not to say anything?'

Sam shook his head. 'Sorry, you know I can't take you with me.'

'I'd be more help than your spiteful little redhead,' Loveday snapped, and immediately regretted the comment. She flashed him an embarrassed look. 'Sorry. I didn't mean that. I'm sure Amanda is a very capable detective.'

'You think you would make a better one,' Sam said sharply. He looked away, angry, but he didn't know if his annoyance was aimed at himself or Loveday — or because she was right. She would make a better detective than Amanda Fox. He couldn't fault the detective's enthusiasm, but her people skills left a lot to be desired. Her abilities to persuade others to confide in her needed some work.

'Well?' Loveday persisted. 'Are we visiting Karrek together?'

'Would it make any difference if I said no?'

Loveday shook her head, laughing. 'I really do promise not to interfere.'

Sam knew he was making a rod for his own back by allowing Loveday to get involved in his investigation, but she was right, Ben and Keri were her friends — and had been long before he'd known them.

He sighed. 'Now let's be quite clear on this. If you come with me to Jamie's boat it's on the strict understanding that we are going there as a favour to Ben. We promised to try and find his friend, Jamie, and that's all we are trying to do.'

Loveday gave an earnest nod. 'I understand. Of course I do. This has nothing to do with your case.'

Sam wasn't sure this was true, but what harm could it do to take a wander over Karrek way on a Sunday morning. At this stage there was no evidence that it was Jamie's body back in the cave. If he was on his boat all hale and hearty, then no harm would be done. If he wasn't there, and still no one had heard from him over the past week, then he was still a missing person. And that would definitely be a concern.

It was almost ten o'clock when they drove through Karrek and turned down towards the creek. An outgoing tide had drained the water, leaving a collection of boats anchored at crazy angles on the mud bed.

Jamie's narrowboat was immediately recognizable. It was the most rundown of all of them in the motley little fleet.

'The *April Rose*,' Loveday said, gazing at the faded red paint. 'Such a lovely name for a boat. I wonder who April was?'

But Sam was silent as they stood together on the bank, looking along the length of the narrowboat. A collection of leggy geranium plants in pots lined the deck, but the doors to the cabin hung on hinges that were in need of repair.

Loveday's gaze took in the peeling varnish and lopsided black chimney. The sad-looking vessel reminded her of an old friend who was in need of a hug.

Neither of them heard the man's approach and they both spun round in surprise when he said, 'Can I help you?'

'We're looking for Jamie,' Sam said. 'Is he around?' His eyes were travelling over the stranger's frayed blue denim shirt and old brown leather waistcoat. The man's jeans were torn and he wore shabby blue deck shoes. His whole dishevelled appearance reminded Sam of a tramp, but his refined tones suggested otherwise.

The man's intelligent grey eyes went from one to the other. 'Jamie isn't here,' he said.

'Do you know where he is?' Loveday threw in quickly, ignoring Sam's scowl.

The wary eyes narrowed. 'Who wants to know?'

Sam cleared his throat. 'Ben Poldavy . . . he asked us to look in on Jamie. I take it this is his boat.'

A sudden movement from the boat had them all spinning round again.

'There's someone on board,' Loveday said.

'It's Maya. She's been keeping an eye on things for Jamie.'

Even as the man spoke a young woman emerged from below deck and stood giving them a questioning stare.

She was a pretty girl with a mass of short brown curls and a fresh, rosy complexion that needed no make-up to enhance it. She looked small, delicate even, in her grey tapestry waistcoat and white shirt. But there was defiance in the business-like way her sleeves were rolled up, and wariness in how she held herself.

'We're looking for Jamie,' Sam called over to her.

'They're friends of Ben,' the man explained.

The girl's green eyes lit up. 'Has Jamie been in touch with you?'

'No, sorry,' Sam said quickly. 'But we would like a word with you if that's all right.'

She nodded, but Loveday could see how her shoulders had slumped. She'd been hoping for good news and they could offer none.

They stepped on board and followed Maya through the hatch, Sam's broad shoulders filling the small gap as they clambered down into the saloon.

Loveday failed to hide her surprise. The living quarters were actually quite cosy. They had stepped into a galley with cooker, sink, fridge, cupboards and all the usual equipment. It continued on into a living area with a table and seating. A small pot-bellied black wood-burner gave the place a cosy feel.

Maya saw Loveday's gaze travel admiringly around the space. 'Jamie wanted to make the interior as pleasant as possible before he and Scobey started on the fabric of the boat,' she explained.

'He's done a good job,' Sam said, turning to Maya. 'I don't think we caught your last name.'

'It's Brookes,' she said, coming forward and offering her hand to each of them in turn.

'I'm Sam and this is Loveday,' he said, glancing round as the man they'd met outside joined them.

'And this is our friend Tom Scobey,' Maya said.

The man gave a sullen nod. 'So, do you have news of Jamie?'

Sam shook his head. 'I'm afraid not. We promised Ben we would look in if we were passing this way. He was hoping you might have heard from Jamie. He says it's been a few days now since he went away.'

'A week,' Maya said. 'It's been a week since Jamie went away.'

'Ben wants to find him . . . to make sure he is OK,' Loveday said gently. 'He asked Sam and me to help.'

She turned to the man. 'So if there is anything you can tell us, Mr Scobey.'

'Just Scobey, no mister,' the man muttered, apparently determined to give away as little information as possible, but Loveday had fixed him with an enquiring smile and he grudgingly relented. 'I'm helping Jamie sort the boat out.'

'Yes, Ben mentioned you both.'

'So Ben hasn't heard from Jamie either,' Maya said. It was a statement rather than a question.

Loveday glanced at Sam. She had

already overstepped the mark. She had promised not to interfere with his questioning and already she was taking over. She flashed him an apologetic smile, but he was looking more thoughtful than annoyed. She had a hundred questions, but fought back the urge to let the journalist in her take over. She had to leave this to Sam.

He had moved across the space to stand leaning against a narrow cupboard, his broad 6ft 2 frame dwarfing Maya and Scobey. He folded his arms and crossed his ankles. It was a relaxed pose that Loveday recognized so well.

'I said we were friends of Ben's,' he started, 'but I'm also a policeman.'

Maya and Scobey's heads snapped up and they stared at him.

Loveday studied their worried faces. Maya was biting her bottom lip, and appeared to be on the verge of tears.

Scobey was frowning, but then he'd been doing that since he first set eyes on them. Loveday imagined she saw a spark of fear in the intelligent eyes. Was it fear for Jamie, or fear of Sam now that he'd revealed he was a policeman?

'Something's happened to him, hasn't it?' Maya said, her voice trembling.

Loveday longed to rush in to assure them that Jamie was bound to be fine, but a pinpoint of chill had begun to settle inside her. Was he fine? Where was he?

'We don't know for sure that anything has happened to Jamie,' Sam said. 'But we did advise Ben to report him missing.'

Scobey's brow creased and he glanced away, his shoulders tensing. Neither Sam nor Loveday missed how uncomfortable the man was looking.

'Did either of you report Jamie missing?'

Scobey never lifted his eyes from the floor.

Maya shook her head. 'We should have done, shouldn't we?'

'Why didn't you?' Sam asked.

Maya and Scobey exchanged a look.

'It was his parents,' the girl began. 'We thought perhaps that he had simply taken off to avoid them.'

'Why would he do that?' Loveday asked.

'Because they're awful. They've been trying to track Jamie down all the time he's been here in Cornwall. They won't leave him alone. This is the only place he felt safe.'

'Safe?' Loveday repeated, thinking what a strange word it was to use.

Maya sighed. 'You don't know them. They're so controlling. They want to run Jamie's life. He just wants to be left alone.'

'But I don't understand why that would stop you reporting him missing, especially as you're so obviously worried about him?' Loveday's brow wrinkled.

'We didn't want the Roscows to know he'd gone off,' Scobey interrupted. 'If we'd gone to the police they would have contacted them.' He glanced at Sam. 'It would have been one of their first ports of call, and then the Roscows would have come down here interfering.'

Maya nodded. 'And that wouldn't exactly please Jamie when he gets back. If his parents discovered he was here in Karrek then Jamie would have to disappear again.'

Loveday looked at Sam. He was frowning. He didn't understand the logic of that any more than she did.

'When was the last time you saw Jamie?' Sam turned to Maya.

'Last Saturday. We were supposed to go to the pub for a meal the next day, but he didn't turn up. I thought he'd just forgotten. He often forgot stuff when he was working on the boat.'

Scobey gave a silent nod and kept his eyes cast down.

Maya went on. 'When he didn't come into the pub I came down here looking for him, but he wasn't here and his bed hadn't been slept in the previous night. At first I was annoyed that he'd sloped off without telling me where he was going, but as the days went on and there was still no word from Jamie, I began to worry.' She looked across at Scobey. 'We both did.'

'You don't live here on the boat with Jamie then?' Sam asked.

Maya shook her head. 'I have my own flat in Helston. I'm only here now in case Jamie comes back.'

Sam's expression gave nothing away, but the words 'in case Jamie comes back' suggested Maya wasn't confident that would happen.

'How did you two meet?' he asked.

'My studies of Cornish antiquities,' Maya said. 'I have a part-time job attached to the museum in Helston.' She turned and took a well-thumbed paperback from a shelf above the tiny sink and handed it to Loveday.

She glanced at the title, *Crossing Time to the Stones*. The cover photograph was the Men-an-Tol, an intriguing Neolithic monument consisting of two upright stones either side of a round stone with a hole in the middle. Similar images were on posters and postcards in gift shops all over Cornwall.

'You wrote this?' Loveday was impressed.

'That's Jamie's copy,' Maya said. 'He was well into it.'

'Have you and Jamie ever visited a fogou at Carn Hendra?' Sam asked, but he hardly needed a response. He already knew the answer.

Maya's large emerald eyes widened.

'We were there a couple of weeks ago. How did you know?'

Loveday's heart had started to thud.

'Do you have a photograph of Jamie?' Sam's expression was grim.

For a few seconds it seemed that Maya's eyes were glued to Sam's face. Loveday could almost see the thoughts filtering through the girl's head.

Maya reached for a large tapestry shoulder bag lying on a bench seat. She rummaged amongst the contents and produced a small passport size photo.

'We took this at one of those machines.' A half smile hovered on her mouth. 'We were fooling around.'

Sam took the photo, gazing at the image of the fresh-faced young man. It was the mass of curly dark hair he recognized, and his heart sank. He could feel the three pairs of eyes on him.

Loveday stepped forward, looking down at the picture in his hand. She needed no confirmation. Sam's grim expression said it all. The body in the fogou was Jamie Roscow.

Maya's eyes searched Sam's face, still

hoping she was misreading what she saw there. She threw a frantic look to Scobey, and then back to Sam. 'Why are you looking at Jamie's photo like that? Have you seen him?'

Loveday could feel her insides shaking. This was one part of Sam's job she definitely didn't envy him.

She saw Maya's face crumple as Sam gently told her they'd found a body, and it could be Jamie.

Scobey caught her as she went down, and Sam rushed forward to help him guide her to a chair. All colour had drained from Maya's face as she tried to focus on the big detective.

'It can't be Jamie,' she said in a small shaky voice. 'It can't be!'

Scobey had also gone deathly pale. Loveday could see he was trembling.

Sam cleared his throat. 'We need someone to identify him,' he said gently.

Maya's eyes flew open in horror. 'I can't do that ... don't ask me to do that.'

Loveday saw Sam's attention switch to Scobey, but she didn't think he looked any more capable of identifying poor Jamie than Maya.

'Don't worry,' Sam said kindly. 'We'll sort something out. Do you have an address for Jamie's parents?'

\* \* \*

They were off the boat and walking back along the path to the car when Sam glanced back. There was no sign of either Scobey or Maya on the deck of *April Rose*. They were still down in the saloon trying to come to terms with their shock.

Loveday tugged his arm. 'You knew all along that it was Jamie's body in the fogou.'

'I didn't,' Sam said. 'But I had a feeling. The photograph confirmed it.'

'I wish you'd warned me. That was a horrible experience. Poor Maya.'

Sam gave a resigned nod and then asked, 'What did you think of Scobey?'

Loveday frowned. She wasn't sure what he meant. 'He looked pretty shattered too,' she said.

They had rounded the bend and were out of sight of the boat. Sam glanced up at the pub that overlooked the creek. 'Fancy a drink?'

The Badger Inn didn't look like the kind of place he would normally have frequented but Loveday knew he was in detective mode.

So she nodded and followed him up the incline to the shabby black and white painted hostelry.

The buzz of conversation stopped as they walked in and the half-dozen drinkers around the bar turned to inspect the newcomers.

Sam nodded a brief, inclusive smile around the room. A couple of the customers nodded back, but most of them had lost interest and were returning to their pints.

'Nice place.' Loveday grimaced, sliding behind a table from where they could watch the comings and goings in the bar, not that much of that was happening at the moment. It was not the sort of pub that would attract visitors.

Having established there was no coffee

on offer, Sam returned from the bar with two tall glasses of orange juice and sat where he could view the drinkers.

'D'you think Jamie was a regular in here?' Loveday asked.

Sam didn't know, but it was something he would find out for sure on his second visit, for he would certainly be returning to Karrek very soon.

Twenty minutes later they'd returned to the car and were driving past the RNAS Culdrose base on the outskirts of Helston when Loveday shot Sam a look. 'Will you have to ask Ben to do the ID now?'

Sam kept his eyes on the road as he nodded. 'I need to see Ben as soon as possible but you don't have to come with me, Loveday. I'll drop you off at the cottage first.'

'No.' Loveday sighed. 'I'd better go with you. Keri will be upset too.'

Relaying the news to Ben and Keri that a body found at the fogou could be Jamie was not going to be easy.

★ ★ ★

The cottage door had opened before they'd even got out of the car. Keri stood there, her eyes full of dread. 'It's bad news, isn't it?' she called across to them.

Loveday hurried forward and touched her friend's arm. 'Is Ben home?' she asked gently.

Keri nodded. 'He's out the back, painting.' They followed her through the cottage to the back garden, where Ben had set up his easel and was painting the lighthouse Loveday could see further along the coast.

All the colour had drained from Keri's face. Loveday put an arm around her. She could feel the girl shaking. The three of them stood in silence as Sam imparted the bad news.

Ben laid down his brush, the bristles still heavy with white paint. His shoulders drooped. Keri shot forward and gathered him into her arms.

'I'm so sorry, Ben,' she said softly, laying her cheek on top of his head.

'Are you sure it's Jamie?' Ben looked up at Sam.

'Pretty certain,' Sam said. 'But we need

someone to identify him to be definite.'

Ben drew a slow, shuddering breath and then nodded. 'I'll do it,' he said.

# 6

Keri was not at her desk when Loveday walked into the editorial office next morning. It was already nine o'clock, but the place looked like the *Mary Celeste*.

Merrick's head came up as she entered the room. He had a phone clamped to his ear as he beckoned her into his office. His room was just a corner of the editorial floor that had been sectioned off with glass panels, but as owner of the *Cornish Folk* magazine, and editor in chief, he was able to be part of the team and remain aloof at the same time. He beckoned Loveday into his office and waved her into the seat opposite him.

'Where is everyone?' she asked, when Merrick finished his call.

'Mylor has gone to Redruth to take pictures of an old mine engine, Ruthie has called in sick, and that was Keri on the phone just now. She told me about Ben's friend. She's gone with him to give her support. Apparently he's pretty upset.'

Loveday sank back into her chair, sighing. 'I think this has been one of the most awful weekends of my life.'

Merrick's look softened. He hated this kind of upset amongst his staff, but it was more than that. Keri and Loveday were his friends. 'Want to talk about it?'

'Probably not . . . oh, I don't know. I'd just be sharing my gloom and making you feel bad as well.'

Merrick managed a crooked smile. 'Share away. I want to help if I can.'

She gave a hopeless shrug. 'Saturday should have been a brilliant day. I'd been so looking forward to it. Sam and I had gone to see the cottage, or at least what was left of it . . . '

'The cottage?'

'Oh, of course. You don't know about my inheritance.' She gave a wry smile. She had been so excited when she and Sam went over there to see it. It didn't matter that it was only a pile of rubble now. She could have rebuilt it. It would have been part of the pleasure. Now it would be tainted forever. Was this why she was so upset about discovering the body? She didn't know.

Merrick listened in silence as Loveday told the story, including her and Sam's visit to Jamie's boat, and meeting his friends, Maya and Scobey. When she'd finished he was still quietly thoughtful.

It was Ben she should be feeling sorry for. At that very moment he could be in the mortuary with Sam, staring at his dead friend's face.

She shuddered, angry with herself for thinking only how all this affected *her*.

Merrick's voice brought her back into the room.

'Are you listening to me, Loveday? None of this was your fault. Bad things happen to good people. You can't take on everybody's pain.' He leaned forward. 'And you're not being selfish, so stop beating yourself up.'

Loveday sucked in her bottom lip to stop it trembling. People being nice to her could still make her cry. She swallowed a lump in her throat and nodded.

'You're right. I'm being stupid but I

feel so helpless. Ben and Keri must be so distressed right now and here's me babbling on.'

But an idea was taking shape in her mind and she was already trying to work out how to execute it as she went back to her desk.

It was eleven before Sam rang to tell her that Ben had identified the body as being Jamie.

'How is he?' she asked.

'Ben's fine now, but seeing Jamie's body was pretty rough on him. I think it helped to have Keri with him.'

Loveday sighed. 'Well, at least we know. What happens now, Sam? Will you tell Maya and Scobey?'

'Will and I are on our way there now,' he said.

The police activity around the fogou had been scaled down since Saturday, but from where she stood, Loveday could see a few people still moving around behind the blue and white tape that marked the crime scene. Her gaze travelled across the rough land, trying to make out the area where her great-aunt's cottage had once stood, but from this distance it was impossible to judge.

She was standing on a rough track, fifty yards from where she had parked the Clio in a clearing. She'd passed the farmhouse a little way back, annoyed with herself for not taking charge of her nerves. Clem Tangye was just an old farmer, but there was something about him that set her teeth on edge.

She glanced back over her shoulder at the squat stone building. The tractor was there, which meant Tangye was probably at home.

Back in the office she had given Merrick a brief outline of a new article she was planning based on Cornwall's standing stones.

Chatting to Clem Tangye seemed like an obvious place to start her research. From what she could remember of their previous encounter the man clearly knew a lot about the fogou, even if he'd tried to pretend that he didn't. Knowledge like that was exactly what she needed, and if she could pick up a few facts about the history of Carn Hendra cottage as well then that would be a bonus. So why was she so reluctant to approach the farmhouse?

She forced her legs to move, to take her back along the rutted track. Her breath was coming in sharp bursts and she focused on that to control the tremble inside her as she stood at Tangye's door and reached for the horseshoe knocker.

It was the old man who opened the door. He narrowed his eyes. 'Yes?' He was giving Loveday a hostile stare.

She cleared her throat. 'Good morning, Mr Tangye. Do you remember me?' She could see that he obviously did, but she went on with her rehearsed approach anyway.

'You helped me find the old cottage I was looking for . . . Carn Hendra.' She had no idea why she deliberately didn't mention Sam.

'I remember yous. I'm not senile,' he snapped. 'What d'you want?'

She began to explain about the magazine and got as far as mentioning her research when Clem Tangye was pushed aside from behind and a small, stout woman with curly grey hair, bright pink cheeks and sharp blue eyes, appeared in his place.

'Pay no heed to him, my love. I don't know where his manners have gone. We don't leave folks standing on the doorstep.' She turned to glare at her husband. 'Not in this house!'

Loveday allowed herself to be ushered into a big comfortable kitchen. A black wood-burning stove glowed in a small inglenook fireplace, even though the May day was fine.

'Sit yourself down, my love, Clem will put the kettle on.' She sent another glare in her husband's direction and the man shuffled off across the kitchen to do as he was told.

'I don't want to put you to any trouble,' Loveday called after him, but the farmer's wife waved away her protest as she settled herself in a chair by the fire and indicated Loveday should take the one opposite.

'So, my lovely, how can we help you?'

Loveday swung round to address her comments to the woman's husband. 'I actually want to pick your brain, Mr

Tangye,' she said. 'As I tried to tell you, I am researching a magazine article about Cornish antiquities and from reading between the lines of what you told me the other day I suspect you know all about the old fogou out there.' She nodded to the window that looked out across the moor.

Clem Tangye had poured three mugs of tea and without enquiring, put milk and sugar in each one and brought them through, placing them on a low table next to Loveday.

He acknowledged his wife's threatening stare. 'OK, what do ee want to know?' His tone was grudging as he scowled back at Lizzie.

'Anything you can tell me about its history,' Loveday said.

'It's a bad place and ee ought not to go there, and that's all ee needs to know.'

After what had happened down there, Loveday understood the comments, but the farmer had warned her and Sam off before they discovered Jamie's body. So what more did he know?

She glanced from husband to wife. 'I'm

assuming you have been here at the farm for some years?'

'I was born here, like my father afore me, and his father afore him,' Tangye said.

Loveday felt a flutter of excitement. 'You must have known my family then. You knew about Carn Hendra cottage . . . '

'Your family?' Mrs Tangye's head shot up. 'Your family lived around here?'

Loveday explained about her inheritance as the woman listened with growing surprise.

'We knew the Tallacks. Why didn't you tell her, Clem?'

Her eyes rounded on Loveday, fixing her with a stare. 'If you own Carn Hendra then you also own that dirty old cave. It's on your family's land.'

She wasn't a hundred per cent sure why she had come here, except that she had to face her fear of this place. But she hadn't been expecting these people to know her family, although if she'd thought about it she would have realized that they were bound to know the Tallacks. Thoughts raced around her mind like express trains. Even with the horror of what had happened in the fogou she had felt drawn to this place, and now there were people who could tell her about her family. She felt a sudden surge of excitement, but this wasn't the time to explore her family tree. There was so much more she wanted to know.

Interfering in Sam's investigation was the last thing on her mind, but a thought had just struck her and she needed some answers.

'Did you know that body was in there, Mr Tangye . . . before we found him, I mean?'

The farmer's wife was staring at her husband. 'You didn't, did you, Clem?'

The man gave a bad-tempered grunt and looked away, blinking rapidly.

'Well, tell us,' the woman persisted, her voice rising. 'Did you know that poor soul was down there?'

Tangye couldn't meet their eyes. His mouth formed a hard line and his shoulders slumped. 'He were dead anyway. There weren't nothing I could've done.'

They both stared at him in shocked silence, and then the man's wife said, 'You found that poor person's body and you didn't tell anybody?' Her eyes were wide with disbelief.

'I told ee. There were nothing to be done,' he snapped. 'The man were dead.'

'You could have given him his dignity. How could you leave him lying down there? How could you do that, Clem?' Lizzie Tangye was becoming more and more upset. 'You have to tell the police.'

'What's the point?' Clem fired back. 'It's all done now. They've found him.'

'They might think you did it, that's the point,' the woman spluttered, and her once pink cheeks were now infused with purple.

'The thing is,' Loveday began carefully, 'you might have left some evidence back there. It would help the police if they could identify that and rule you out, otherwise it is just going to confuse things.'

She had another thought. 'Did you know the man in the fogou?'

Tangye shook his head. 'Not know him,

79

no. He came here weeks ago with a young woman. I told your mate ... the policeman chap. The one that's dead came here, and he left again. I didn't kill him!'

'Then your wife is right. You must tell the police that,' Loveday said.

She drove back to Truro feeling she had opened a can of worms. Tangye still had to explain what he'd been doing in the fogou, but that was for Sam to discover. She would have enough trouble explaining why she'd visited the man in the first place.

# 7

Sam knew Maya and Scobey were probably expecting the worst and might have prepared themselves, but it wouldn't lessen their distress. He was back in the saloon of the *April Rose* with Will, his solemn expression confirming everything before he had even uttered a word.

'It's Jamie, isn't it,' Maya said flatly.

Sam nodded. 'He was identified this morning. I'm so sorry.'

Will stayed silent, studying the man in the corner. The body language was hard to read, but his sour expression was real enough, like it was fixed in stone. It crossed his mind that this man might know — or at least suspect — who might have killed Jamie Roscow. And that was more than they did because so far, they didn't have a clue.

'Can you tell me again about the last time you saw Jamie?' Sam asked gently.

Maya had sunk onto a chair, a

crumpled hankie screwed into her hand. But she wasn't crying.

'It was a week last Saturday, the day before we were due to meet in the pub.'

'What pub was that?' he interrupted, but he already knew.

Maya nodded towards the village. 'The Badgers. Jamie went there all the time.'

'You were about to recall the last time you and Jamie were together?' Sam reminded.

Maya ran the tip of her tongue over her lips and swallowed. 'We had gone to the library in St Just. They have a great archive there for anyone interested in standing stones in West Cornwall. Jamie got the bug from me . . . the research thing I mean.' A smile quivered at the corners of her mouth as she remembered that last day.

'I'm passionate about discovering all I can about Cornwall's antiquities.' She looked up at Sam. 'I'm writing another book about them. Once Jamie got into it he was just as passionate as me.'

Sam glanced across at Will, giving him the nod to take over the questioning.

'How was he that last day?' Will asked. 'Did he seem distant or worried about anything?'

'No, not at all. If anything, he was excited.'

'Excited?' Will repeated.

Maya nodded. 'Jamie was enthusiastic about everything.'

'But you said excited,' Sam cut in.

'He was,' she said slowly. 'I didn't think anything about it at the time, but going over it now, he did seem hyped up about something.'

Sam threw Will a look to continue, but he would make it his business to discover what that was all about. He'd switched his attention to Scobey. He hadn't uttered a word but Sam could tell he was taking everything in. He wondered just how good a friend the two had been to each other. According to Ben, Scobey was just an acquaintance who had been helping Jamie refurbish his boat. He was now wondering if there was more to that friendship.

Will wheeled round, raising an eyebrow at the man. 'What about you, Mr Scobey?

Can you shed any light on why Jamie would have been excited that day?'

Scobey shrugged, but his sour expression didn't alter, making Will wonder if it was a permanent fixture.

'Jamie never confided in me,' he said.

Sam saw Maya's head snap up, and from the look on her face the man's answer had surprised her. But she said nothing.

'How did you two meet?' Sam asked.

'At Helston Library. I was returning a book and Jamie had requested it. We got talking.' She smiled. 'He suggested going for a coffee. We found this little place round the corner, and were still there talking an hour later. I'd never met anyone like Jamie. He just kind of got everything. There was no need to explain myself to him because he always understood where I was coming from.' Her large sad eyes looked away. 'We were on the same wavelength, Jamie and me,' she said, her voice now so quiet she could have been speaking to herself.

Sam had to steel himself against his compassion for this girl. She looked so vulnerable and alone, but she wasn't alone. Scobey was here. The fact that he was on the boat when he and Will arrived meant there was a connection. And now he had moved forward to put a comforting hand on Maya's shoulder. If she needed looking after then this man would be there for her.

'What about you, Mr Scobey? How do you know Jamie?'

'We met in the pub,' he said. 'I'm in there most nights. Jamie came in and sat in a corner nursing a half pint of cider. We all knew who he was. In a place like this he could hardly hide the fact that he was living down on the creek on an old rundown narrowboat.

'I'd been telling Seth Vingoe, the landlord, about a boat I'd been working on over by Porthleven. Jamie must have overheard because he came across and asked if I'd like to make a bit of money?'

Sam understood. 'He wanted you to help him with the boat?'

Scobey nodded, his craggy face still expressionless as he looked around him. 'I didn't realize how much work there was.

The boat was a wreck, hardly worth saving, but Jamie was determined to make something of it.'

'I take it you have some experience of building boats?' It was Will.

'I dabble.'

'Is that how you make your living?' Will continued.

'I help people out . . . do a bit of this and that. It's enough to get me by.'

Sam had been studying the man as he spoke. He'd taken his hand from Maya's shoulder, but he was still standing behind her. Scobey's shabby clothes looked clean enough, but his khaki cotton waistcoat was streaked with white paint and his jeans were threadbare at the knees. Like the previous time Sam had met him, the man's crinkly mousey brown hair was tied back in a stubby ponytail.

Nothing about his appearance suggested he had a private income, and yet . . .

'Where do you live, Mr Scobey?' Sam asked.

'You would have passed the track to my place on the way down. It swings off to the left as you approach the village.'

Out of the corner of his eye, Sam was aware of Will jotting down the information in his little notebook.

'Have you contacted Jamie's parents?' Maya asked.

Scobey's shoulders stiffened, and Sam saw the muscles of his neck working. Or had he imagined that, for there had been no change in the man's stony expression?

'That's all in hand,' Sam said.

'I suppose that means they'll be coming down here?' Maya's voice was flat.

'I don't know,' Sam said. He was still watching Scobey, but his expression was giving nothing away. If he had any reservations about the Roscows, he was keeping his thoughts to himself.

Sam handed his card to each of them as he and Will left, making sure they had Maya's mobile number in return. Scobey said he didn't have a phone, mobile or otherwise.

As the detectives walked back along the banks of the creek, Sam again glanced back at the boat. Scobey had come up on deck and was staring after them.

'Fancy a pint, Will?' he said, still watching the gaunt-looking figure on the *April Rose*. 'I think it's time I renewed my acquaintance with that pub.'

The Badger Inn didn't seem to have improved since his last visit with Loveday. The squat stone building had a slate roof and must once have had blue painted windows, but that was before years of sun, rain and the sharp Cornish winds had got to work on them. Two rusty metal seats were positioned either side of the open door next to large plastic containers of woody shrubs that were choked with weeds.

'Some state.' Will tutted, running his gaze over the miserable building. His nose turned up in distaste.

'I doubt if its less than impressive kerb appeal will harm the beer,' Sam said.

They ducked their heads and adjusted their eyes to the darkened interior as they went into the bar. Four heads turned in their direction as their owners examined them with silent interest. Sam wondered if any of the drinkers would recognize him from his last visit.

The overweight barman wasn't the one who had served him before. He moved the podgy arm that was resting on the sticky bar top. 'What can I get you gents?'

Sam glanced at Will. 'A pint?'

Will nodded and Sam ordered two pints of a local craft beer before turning to smile at the others standing at the bar. 'Morning,' he said. Three heads nodded in unison.

'Not local then, are you?' This from the small wizened man in the middle.

Sam suspected they all knew exactly who Will and he were, and why they were here. News travelled fast in villages like this, but he just smiled and said, 'No, not local.'

He handed over a £10 note for the drinks, and the landlord turned to ring the sale up in the till before placing the change on the counter. He looked from one to the other, wasting no time in getting to the point.

'You'll be here about young Roscow,' he said.

Sam took his time lifting his beer and

savouring the first sip, knowing all eyes were on him.

'Is it right he's been done in?' This from his second but one neighbour at the bar.

Sam wiped the beer froth from his mouth with the back of his hand. 'And you are?' he said, turning to look at the man.

'Jake Carter.' He nodded towards the door. I live just up the hill,' he informed him, as though this gave him permission for the question.

'You knew Jamie Roscow?'

The man nodded again.

'We all knew Jamie,' the landlord said, and stuck out his hand. 'Seth Vingoe,' he introduced himself. 'I own this place.' He paused. 'It's true then. Jamie's dead?'

'I'm afraid so,' Sam said, pulling out his warrant card as Will followed suit. 'Anything you can tell us about him might be useful. I gather he was popular.'

The barman sighed. 'Young Jamie spent a lot of time in here. He was nice enough, but he kept himself to himself if you know what I mean.'

A chorus of agreement went round the bar.

'Nothing not to like, no airs and graces about Jamie,' said the man who'd introduced himself as Jake.

'How long had he been in the village?' Will asked, although they both already knew the answer.

The man at the far end of the bar said, 'More'n a year I reckon.' He glanced round at his fellow drinkers for confirmation, and they all nodded.

'Funny though,' said the man next to Sam. 'He had this highfalutin accent, but wasn't a snob.'

'No,' Jake agreed, not like his mate up the hill. That one's full of himself.'

'Who's that?' Sam asked.

The man glanced at the barman, who threw back a warning frown.

'Just because he's a customer of yours doesn't mean we have to be nice about him. Allen's a pain in the arse and you know it, Seth.'

'Allen who?' Will asked.

'Walter Allen, another one from

London, but no breeding with him. Total fraud ... always talking down to the likes of us.'

His fellow drinkers nodded in unison again, and he continued, 'Walter's a writer. He's got the big house up on the ridge there. Hillcrest it's called.'

Will had pulled out his notebook and was getting it all down.

'But if you're thinking of paying him a visit, he won't be there,' Jake said. 'Only comes down at weekends.'

'You mentioned he was a special friend of Jamie's?'

'Well, *he* thought he was,' Jake said. 'But Jamie could see right through him. The bloke's a total fraud.'

The man next to Sam, who identified himself as Harry Dunstan, piped up. 'He latched on to Jamie, always trying to get him and his girlfriend to go for meals with him.'

'Never invited us for no meals,' the third man, who gave his name as Giles Drew, shook his head. 'The likes of us wasn't posh enough for likes of him.'

'You said Mr Allen was a writer?' Sam

asked, before taking another deep draught of beer.

Seth the barman turned to grab a dog-eared paperback from the back of the bar. 'That's him.' He tapped the book's garish front cover. 'Desmond Height.'

Sam racked his brain, trying to think if he recognized the name. Loveday almost certainly would.

He opened the book. There was an inscription. 'To my friend, Jamie — an ever open mind.'

'This is Jamie's copy?' Sam raised an eyebrow.

The barman smiled. 'I don't think he even read it. He left it here for any customers who were interested.'

Sam flicked through the pages. Judging by the condition of the book, plenty folk had been interested.

'You can keep it if you like,' Seth said. 'I reckon everybody that wanted to read it will have flicked through it enough.'

The tide had seeped back into the creek while they were inside, but the pungent smell of damp mud was still being carried on the wind. They retraced their steps until they could see the narrowboat again. Will wrinkled his nose.

'Not the most charming smell in the world, is it?' he said, his gaze travelling downstream to where the *April Rose* was now floating free.

Sam noted Scobey had come out onto the deck and was looking in their direction. He wondered if the man had been keeping an eye on them, waiting for them to leave the village.

'Where to now, boss?' Will said, not taking his eye off the creek.

'Let's chance our luck and try checking up on our crime-writing friend. He might be home. I don't suppose he takes the locals into his confidence about his comings and goings.'

# 8

Loveday sipped the red wine Sam had brought home with him that evening as she watched him eat, dreading the moment when she'd have to reveal she'd visited the Tangye's farm. He wouldn't be pleased, but he'd have to know that the old man had discovered Jamie's body in the fogou — and said nothing about it.

'Ben was more upset than I'd been expecting,' Sam said, a forkful of chicken on its way to his mouth. 'Did Keri say anything today?'

Loveday had been feeling bad about not getting in touch with her friend. She had no idea why she hadn't called Keri, except that she had wanted to distance herself from the whole horrible business. What was happening to her?

She looked away from Sam's puzzled expression, pushing her half-eaten meal away.

'OK.' Sam sighed, putting down his

cutlery and narrowing his eyes at her. 'Are you going to tell me what's wrong?'

'I'm a rubbish friend, that's what's wrong. I've let Keri and Ben go through all this on their own. I've given them absolutely no support.'

Sam got up and wrapped his arms around her. 'You're still upset about Saturday,' he said gently. 'You had a terrible shock finding that body. Don't be so hard on yourself, Loveday. Why don't you ring Keri now? She'll be waiting to hear from you.'

He was right. She had to call Keri, but she wasn't sure her friend would even want to speak to her after she had so shamefully neglected her and Ben.

Loveday wondered if Sam would still be so nice to her when she told him what she'd learned from Tangye that afternoon. Ringing Keri now was only going to delay it, but her friend was more important now than her feelings. She reached for her mobile phone and punched in the number, biting her lip impatiently as she heard it ringing out.

'Loveday, I was just thinking about

you.' Keri was sounding breathless. For some reason that made Loveday feel guiltier than ever.

She said, 'I should have called sooner, I'm so sorry. How are you both?'

Keri sighed. 'It's been a pretty horrible day, but we're getting through it. Ben's still very quiet. He was fond of Jamie.' She paused, and then said quietly, 'Such a waste.'

'Sam will find who did this to Jamie. I promise you, Keri.'

'It won't bring Jamie back though, will it? I keep thinking of his poor girlfriend.'

'You can't take everyone's sorrows on your own shoulders, Keri.'

Loveday wasn't expecting the laugh at the other end of the phone. 'But isn't that exactly what you do, Loveday? I've never met anyone who got herself so involved in other people's lives.'

'Are you telling me off for being nosey?' There was amusement in Loveday's voice.

'Of course not, but you do get yourself into some tight corners.'

Loveday couldn't deny that. She was

still trying to work out how to tell Sam that she had gone to the Tangye's farm earlier.

She could hear Ben's voice in the background.

'He's asking how you are,' Keri said.

'I'm fine. It's you two who are important.'

'We'll look after each other. Don't worry about us. It was good to hear from you though, Loveday.'

Keri was beginning to sound like her old self and Loveday found herself smiling. 'You, too,' she said.

She went slowly back to the sitting room.

Sam had brought her wine glass through. She was sipping her drink and about to launch into her Clem Tangye story when Sam slid a book in front of her. It was a tatty looking paperback of a cheap crime novel. She frowned at it, recognizing the author's name.

'I wouldn't have thought Desmond Height was your kind of thing, Sam.'

He raised an eyebrow. 'You've heard of him?'

'He's a best-selling crime novelist; of course I've heard of him. But I've never read any of his books.'

She turned the scruffy paperback over and glanced at the blurb on the back cover. 'I don't know this one though. Where did you get it?'

'It was given to me. What can you tell me about Height?'

Loveday raised her eyes and studied the ceiling, trying to remember what she knew about the writer.

'He's won a few awards for popular crime fiction. I'd have to Google him about which ones. Why do you want to know?'

'It's a name that came up today.'

'Connected to Jamie Roscow?'

Sam gave her a patient frown and she put up her hands in defence. 'Just asking. I'm not trying to poke my nose into your case.' She took a deep breath before glancing back up at him. Sam was already giving her one of his looks.

'OK, Loveday. What's going on?'

She frowned. He wasn't going to like what she was about to say, but there was no point in delaying it further. She took another steadying breath.

'I went to see Clem Tangye today.'

She was carefully avoiding his eyes, but she could tell he was frowning at her.

'Go on,' he said quietly.

'I'm researching a new feature for the magazine and needed information about Cornish standing stones, places of ancient ritual . . . fogous.' Her voice trailed to a whisper.

She still didn't dare look at him. The explosion would come at any second. She waited, but he remained silent. She closed one eye and squinted up at him. His look of fury shocked her.

'You're annoyed with me. I wasn't interfering in your case, really I wasn't, Sam.'

'So what exactly *were* you doing? Have you any idea how much this kind of thing impacts on my work, Loveday? For pity's sake, it looks like we are working together. You're not supposed to get involved. You promised not to do this again.'

'It wasn't on purpose,' she said lamely, running both hands over her long hair and pushing it back from her face.

'I also wanted to ask him about Carn Hendra. The Tangyes have lived there for years, I thought they might have known my family.'

She waited for Sam to ask if they did, but he said nothing.

Loveday fidgeted with her empty glass before stealing another look at him. He still looked angry. She took a deep breath.

'Tangye told me something else, Sam.'

She waited until she had his attention before saying, 'He knew Jamie's body was in the fogou . . . before we found him, I mean.'

Sam stared at her. He was looking more outraged than ever, and then raised his hand. 'Wait a minute. Let's scroll back here. Clem Tangye told you he found the body and didn't report it?'

Loveday gave a bleak nod.

'But . . . why?'

'You'll have to ask him that.'

But Sam was already on his mobile. She heard him ordering one of his team to pick up Clem Tangye and put him in a holding cell.

'You're arresting him?' she asked, surprised.

'He'll be helping us with our enquiries,' Sam retorted grimly. 'And I want to give him time to think long and hard about that.'

# 9

'Sam left early this morning,' Cassie called out over the drum of Loveday's running shower. Her friend's reply was an indecipherable muffle. Cassie plugged in the kettle and reached into the cupboard for a couple of coffee mugs. The toast was also on the table when Loveday came through towelling her hair dry.

'I was asking because I saw him taking off up the drive like a bat out of hell,' Cassie said.

'Sam's got a busy day, that's all,' Loveday said, but he'd left her in no doubt last night that he hadn't appreciated her visit to the Tangyes' farm. She thought about sharing it with Cassie, but she would probably take Sam's side, so she tried changing the subject.

'I really appreciate you coming by to make my breakfast, Cassie.' She tossed down the damp towel and sat at the table, helping herself to a piece of toast. 'But what exactly are you doing here?'

'Do I need a reason to visit a friend?'

'Of course not.' Loveday grinned. 'But I don't usually get the pleasure of your company before eight in the morning.'

'Adam and I are taking the kids to Disneyland, Paris for a few days. We're leaving in an hour, but I wanted a word with you before we left.' Cassie brushed the toast crumbs from the side of her mouth with a delicate pinkie. 'I've been thinking about that cottage of yours. Have you thought about what you're going to do with it?'

Loveday frowned. 'Sadly, it's not exactly a cottage, more a small mountain of stones.'

'But it's your mountain of stones.' Cassie's eyes were shining. 'You can rebuild the place.'

'You haven't seen the mountain,' Loveday said. 'It's a complete ruin.'

'But if you own the land . . . '

'No.' Loveday shook her head. 'Even if I did have it built up again, it's in the middle of nowhere. It's not as if I could ever live there.'

'I'm not suggesting you should, but you could sell it, or rent it . . . or something. Where's your entrepreneurial spirit?'

'I don't know . . . ' Loveday sighed.

'You could think of it as saving your family's former home. Don't you think they would love that? It could be like a project.'

'I don't need a project.'

'Well, that's fine,' Cassie said. 'All I'm saying is just don't rule it out.'

The idea was still going round and round in Loveday's head as she drove to Truro an hour later.

The sight of Keri back at her computer as she walked in brought a smile to her face.

'So,' she grinned, dumping her shoulder bag on her desk. 'All present and correct again?'

Keri gave a silly salute and smiled back. 'Yes, everything's fine. Yesterday was horrible, but we're coming to terms with it. Ben's still upset about Jamie, but he's managing it.'

Loveday nodded. 'He just needs to give it time. Can't be an easy thing to come to terms with.' She was remembering her own feelings on finding the body, and she hadn't even known the man.

'Actually, I have a favour to ask.' Keri gave Loveday an appealing look. 'Ben's got a painting that Jamie did. He wants his girlfriend to have it, but we don't know how to contact her.'

'She's living on Jamie's boat,' Loveday said, and then felt like kicking herself. She could sense what was coming — and it did.

'We did wonder.' Keri's eyes slid down to her desk drawer. 'I've brought the painting with me. I don't suppose you would come with me?'

*'Sorry, but no . . . definitely not.'* The words were on the tip of her tongue, so why hadn't she said them? What would be so wrong with doing a friend a favour? What harm could it do to see Jamie's girlfriend again? It wasn't as though she was planning to get involved in Sam's case. And he hadn't said the woman was off limits.

Keri slid Jamie's artwork out of her desk drawer and handed it to Loveday.

She studied it. The picture had been painted on hardboard and appeared to be a rather heavy-handed effort. It was the inside of the Badger Inn, complete with customers around the bar. The colours were treacly dark and the brushstrokes careless and heavy. Even to her inexperienced eye it looked crude.

'What does Ben think of this?' she asked, tilting her head and squinting at the painting.

'I don't know, he hasn't said.' Keri shrugged. 'But it's not exactly a work of art, is it? Beats me why would anyone would want to paint the inside of a pub, and not a particularly attractive one.'

Loveday frowned. 'Maybe he was practising character studies.' Her glance moved along the line of drinkers at the bar but the features were indistinguishable. Some of these people had likely been in the pub when she and Sam had called in that day, only she couldn't recognize any of them. She paused. Maybe she did recognize one of the drinkers. She was remembering the picture of Desmond Height, aka Walter

Allen on the back of the trashy detective novel Sam had given her. Could the solitary figure at the far end of the bar be Walter Allen?

It made sense. Why else would Sam be showing an interest in him if he wasn't connected to the murder in some way? Jamie had painted the man with a wine glass halfway to his mouth. And there was something about his eyes — a strange look. She slipped her hand into her bag and pulled out her mobile phone, snapping off a couple of pictures of the painting.

It wasn't exactly a pretty picture. Loveday wasn't sure Jamie's girlfriend would even want it.

She was still weighing up the sense of agreeing to accompany Keri as they drove into Karrek, and made their way down to the creek.

★ ★ ★

The old farmer sat slumped in his chair across the table from Sam and Will in the interview room. His night in the cells had left him dishevelled and defeated-looking.

A jab of guilt was creeping into Sam's head as he watched the old man. Had he been right to have him arrested, or had he only done that because he'd been angry with Loveday? No, he wasn't that unprofessional ... but still, the man didn't look well.

'Can we get you anything, Mr Tangye? A glass of water?'

'You can get me out of here. I've done nothing wrong.'

Sam nodded to the young uniformed officer in the room and mouthed 'water' and the officer slipped out to find some.

'You know why you're here,' Sam said, studying the grey crumpled face.

Tangye didn't look at him.

'You found Jamie Roscow's body and you didn't tell anyone. Why would you do that?'

No reply.

Sam pursed his lips and narrowed his eyes.

'Did you put him in there, Clem?'

But even as he said it he knew the old man could never have had the strength to do that. He could have lured Jamie into the fogou though and smashed his head in. It hadn't been a considered attack. It had the look of a frenzied act, maybe by a killer who was panicking.

Tangye swallowed, but his eyes stayed firmly cast down.

The two detectives waited.

The farmer sighed. 'OK, so I should have told somebody. I . . . I didn't want the wife to know I still went down there.'

Sam and Will exchanged a look.

'Why not?' Will asked.

'Because I promised, didn't I. I promised Lizzie I would stay away from the place. If I'd said about that poor young chap being dead in there I would have given myself away.'

Will's frown deepened. 'I don't understand. Why did you promise not to go down the cave?'

The man's look of irritated disbelief travelled from one officer to the other, and then he shook his head. He clearly thought both men were idiots.

'Because of *her* of course . . . Chrissie.'

Sam blinked, not quite sure what the

man was telling them.

But Tangye was on a roll now. He went on, 'It might have been forty years ago, and Chrissie might be long gone now for all I know, but it doesn't stop my missus from being jealous.' He shook his head. 'Nearly threw me out she did. Never did see a woman so mean.'

Sam stared at him, trying to make sense of what he was hearing, and failing.

'You'll have to do a bit better than that, Clem. Why was your wife jealous?'

Tangye's brow went into deep furrows and his keen grey eyes stared at them from under a line of shaggy white eyebrows.

'I thought you detective people were supposed to be smart? The old fogou is where we used to go . . . Chrissie and me. It was our special place.' The eyes clouded over. The old man was back in the past. He was remembering another time — a time when he was young, and in love.

'Nobody ever went there you see,' he went on. 'We had a proper little nest inside . . . candles, blankets.' He gave an embarrassed cough, his grey pallor turning pink. 'Everything we needed.'

Will glanced across to Sam, who indicated he should stay quiet.

Clem Tangye was in his own little world now as memories of his exciting, clandestine affair flooded his mind. He gave a wistful smile and for a fleeting moment he looked twenty years younger.

'We weren't harming anyone. It was only a little dalliance. We knew it couldn't last. Chrissie had no intention of leaving her Jacob, and Lizzie and I were happily married — still are even after all these years. It was only a bit of fun with Chrissie and me, but Jacob found out. He'd followed her to the fogou one day and waited outside for a while before coming in.'

His face creased into a painful grimace as he remembered. 'Caught us at it, he did.' Another embarrassed cough. 'I thought he was going to kill the both of us, but he did worse than that. He marched off and told my Lizzie.'

Sam was trying to imagine this old man as the Casanova he was trying to paint himself. He tilted his head and squinted at the farmer. He could just about see it. Out of the corner of his eye he could also see Will trying to conceal a grin. He sat back, folding his arms.

'OK, Clem, so who was your lady friend? We need her full name.'

'She's gone . . . probably dead now. I told you.'

'Her name, Clem.'

'She was Chrissie Daniel, but I always knew her as Chrissie Tallack. She and her old mother, Martha lived out at Carn Hendra.'

Sam's heart skipped a beat. Suspicions had started to creep into his mind as soon as Tangye had started his story, but the idea had seemed so ridiculous that he discounted it. Now he didn't know what to believe. Family skeletons! It was almost funny. He hoped Loveday would think so when he told her — and he would have to tell her.

'If this little liaison of yours happened forty years ago, and you believe the lady involved is no longer with us, then why are you still going back to the fogou?'

Will took the words out of Sam's mouth. They both waited as the man shrugged.

'I go there for a smoke.'

Both detectives raised an eyebrow.

'Lizzie doesn't know I still have the odd smoke, and what she don't know won't harm her.' He sighed. 'But she'll find out now, won't she?' He gave them a pleading look. 'She doesn't really need to know about the smokes, does she?'

'How else would you explain your visits to the fogou?' Will asked.

'Visit! She only needs to know about that one visit. I could say I'd been checking up on the safety of the thing. We've had a lot of rain up there. It could cause subsidence.'

Sam frowned and shook his head. The man had it all worked out. From what he'd seen of Mrs Tangye, she wasn't as gullible as the farmer thought.

'Good luck with that,' Sam said.

Tangye straightened up, eyes hopeful.

'Does that mean I can go?'

Sam nodded.

'For the time being, but we may need

to speak to you again.'

He nodded to the young constable who had brought the bottle of water. 'See that Mr Tangye gets a lift home.'

The old man quickly shuffled to his feet and headed for the door. As he reached it, Sam said, 'Just one more thing.'

Tangye turned.

'Has anyone else been asking about the fogou lately?'

Clem Tangye screwed up his eyes. 'Only that writer chap.'

'Writer?'

'Aye, the one that writes that crime stuff. The wife reads them.' He sucked in his bottom lip searching his mind for the man's name. He snapped his fingers. 'Height! That's it . . . Desmond Height.'

\* \* \*

The boat they could see sitting at a lopsided angle in the mud didn't even look safe. Keri glanced up and down the creek hopeful of spying another possibility, but the battered looking *April Rose* was the only narrowboat in sight. 'Surely that's not it?'

'That's it,' Loveday said. She was already regretting being here. 'You go down and hand over the picture. I'll wait in the car.'

But as she turned to go, a voice called out to them, 'Can I help you?'

'I'm a friend of Jamie's — at least my partner, Ben was,' Keri called back, holding up the painting wrapped in brown paper. 'If you're Maya, I have something for you.'

The young woman on the boat lifted a hand to shield her eyes from sun, and then she recognized Loveday. 'Oh, it's you. You'd better come on board then.'

Keri threw Loveday an appealing look. 'Come with me. I feel kind of funny doing this on my own.'

Loveday opened her mouth to decline, but what harm could it possibly do? She didn't even need to tell Sam about this. It had nothing to do with Jamie's murder. She smiled and followed Keri down to the boat.

'You live here?' Keri said, her eyes moving around the surprisingly well-organized space.

The young woman followed her gaze. 'I don't actually, but it's not that bad.' She glanced away, trying to hide the prick of tears. 'It's Jamie's boat. I get comfort from being here.'

'This is my friend, Keri,' Loveday introduced.

The girl took Keri's extended hand. 'I'm Maya Brookes. Jamie and I were . . . friends.'

Keri offered up her package. 'Jamie painted this. Ben thought you would like to have it.'

Maya took the painting and her eyes really did fill up now as she unwrapped it. This time she made no effort to control the flow of tears. She backed away, sinking onto a chair.

Loveday stepped forward. 'Are you all right?' She glanced around her. 'Can I get you anything?'

Maya flipped a hand at them, struggling to regain her composure. 'Can you bring Jamie back?'

'I'm so sorry,' Loveday said. 'I wish we could.'

Maya's eyes travelled back to the painting. 'Did Jamie really do this?'

Keri nodded. 'Ben said he came to our cottage with a sketch that he wanted to turn into a painting. He asked Ben to help him.' She glanced at the painting. 'Do you recognize the place?'

Maya nodded. 'It's the pub, the Badgers. Jamie and I used to go there, it's just up the hill.'

'He must have liked the place a lot to paint it,' Keri said.

'We went there because it was convenient. I wouldn't say either of us particularly liked it.'

'Can you recognize any of the customers?' Loveday asked. It was a shot in the dark, but she might be lucky.

Maya took another glance. 'Only Walter. He always sits there at the end of the bar. That way he can watch everybody and listen in to all the gossip without actually having to join the company. Not that he was encouraged to join in. Walter Allen is not the most popular man in Karrek.'

Loveday could feel a surge of excitement. She was right. It was the author — and he lived right here in this village.

'Why is that?' she asked.

'He's not a nice person, and his wife's even worse, not that she makes many appearances down here in Cornwall. She's a highflying London woman. She owns the publishing company that produces Walter's books.'

Loveday was tempted to ask her name, but she didn't want to appear too interested. It was easy enough to check the woman out online later.

Maya was still looking at the painting. 'I think Jamie was the only one who actually spoke to Walter.' She shook her head. 'But why he even gave him the time of day I can't imagine.'

'Is this Walter Allen a famous author then?' Keri asked, wondering why she had never heard of him.

'Infamous, more like,' Maya said. 'He writes nasty detective novels under the name of Desmond Height.'

'And he lives here in Karrek?' Keri continued.

Loveday stifled a smile. Her friend was doing her job for her.

'He has a house up on the hill,' Maya said. 'But he's usually only here at weekends. He lives in London.'

She stood up. The visit was at an end. Maya obviously wanted to be alone with her memories.

Loveday touched her arm. 'We understand what a terrible time this must be for you, Maya, but you don't have to go through it on your own. Keri and I can be contacted at the offices of the *Cornish Folk* magazine in Truro any time at all.'

Keri nodded. Loveday slid a card from the inside pocket of her denim jacket.

'Ring if there's anything we can do.'

Maya swallowed a lump in her throat. 'Thank you,' she said, taking the card.

# 10

Sam and Will sat in the battered Vauxhall pool car studying the elegant row of front doors along Edmonton Crescent.

'You sure we put the right address in the sat nav, boss? These houses look like the embassies you see on the box.'

Sam shifted his gaze from the curve of the dazzling white properties with their ornate black wrought iron balconies and pots of manicured bay trees, to give Will one of his looks.

'Sorry, just asking,' Will said. 'If this is the kind of high living you get from writing books maybe you and I are in the wrong business.'

'SW postcodes in London don't come cheap,' Sam said, but Will was right. Even by best-selling author standards this was quite a place.

'Curtains are twitching, boss. I think the local Neighbourhood Watch has gone into overdrive.'

'Are you surprised?' Sam said, stepping out onto the footpath and zapping on the car lock. 'This is Mercedes land. These people have probably never seen a rust heap like this in their elegant crescent.'

Will pushed the polished brass bell and a discreet ding-dong sounded from somewhere inside. No response, so the second time he kept his thumb on the button until hurried footsteps were heard inside. The door opened, and a young woman in a black and white maid's uniform gazed enquiringly at them.

Sam smiled. 'We've come to see Mr Allen.'

A troubled look flitted across the young face.

'They're at dinner, sir,' she said. 'Could you call back later?'

'We won't keep him long.' Sam and Will produced their ID and the maid's eyebrow lifted as she glanced at their warrant cards.

'Of course, please come in.' She stepped back for them to enter the smart red-carpeted hall and showed them into an even larger front room, leaving them to gape at the unashamed display of wealth as she disappeared with Sam's card in her hand.

Sam hadn't got much further than the first few pages of Allen's book, but the setting in the filthy back alley of Manchester was a far cry from these surroundings.

It was five minutes before the writer appeared. Sam took a moment to study him. The man was tall, thin, silver-haired and elegant. He wore a cream dinner jacket, black trousers and a red bow tie.

He moved across the carpeted room with the grace of a gazelle and flicked open an ornate box on the mantelpiece. He helped himself to a cigarette, lighting it from a silver lighter that he took from his pocket, before turning to them.

'So, gentlemen, how can I help you?' The voice was refined and sounded arrogant. Sam had to stop himself from flinching. He said, 'We understand you knew a young man, Jamie Roscow?'

Allen lowered the cigarette and squinted at them through the cloud of smoke he had created.

'What do you mean . . . knew? Has something happened to Jamie?'

Sam gave him a serious stare.

'Bad news I'm afraid, Mr Allen. Jamie's dead.'

He watched Allen's face turning several shades of grey.

'That's not possible,' Allen said, stubbing out the half smoked cigarette in a nearby ashtray. 'I was speaking to him a few days ago.'

Sam stifled a sigh. Why did people insist a murder victim was alive when the police told them the opposite? The fact that they had recently seen the deceased hardly explained it.

'When exactly did you last see Jamie Roscow, sir?'

'At my house in Cornwall, that's where I live when I'm not here.' He reached for another cigarette. 'Forgive me, this is such a shock. Jamie was fine last time I saw him.'

'You said a few days ago,' Sam said. 'When exactly?'

Walter Allen's brows came together in a frown and he glanced away. Was he trying to come up with a story or was he genuinely trying to remember? Sam was keeping an open mind.

'Must have been the weekend before last,' he said.

'So, more than a few days ago,' Will commented. 'Can you tell us where exactly you saw him?'

The writer shrugged. 'Nothing to tell. Jamie often drops by . . . used to drop by,' he corrected himself.

'You were friends?' Will chimed in again.

Yes . . . great friends,' Allen mumbled distractedly. 'What happened? How did he die?'

'Sorry, sir. We are not at liberty to say yet,' Sam said. 'Can you tell us how you two knew each other?'

'Jamie had an interest in writing, and when he realized who I was he made it his business to get to know me.'

He threw back his head and puffed out another cloud of cigarette smoke. 'It's very flattering to get that kind of adoration, Detective Inspector — even at my level of fame.'

'Did you meet Jamie anywhere else other than at your house?'

Allen's eyebrows came together again as he thought about this.

'We met in the pub, well everyone in Karrek does that sooner or later.'

Sam nodded. 'Nowhere else?'

'No. Like where?'

Sam ignored the question, but tiny beads of sweat were beginning to break out on Allen's brow.

'Did you know Jamie was also interested in painting?'

'Yes. He was quite talented actually.'

Was it Sam's imagination or had Allen noticeably relaxed?

'Jamie actually painted my house, Hillcrest.' He smiled. 'It's still up on the wall in my study in Karrek.'

Will had been listening to Sam's questions without comment. Now he took his cue from the hardly noticeable nod of his superior officer's head.

He looked Allen in the eyes. 'Do you know Jamie's parents?'

A pause. 'I've met them. I don't know them.'

Will and Sam waited.

Allen sighed. 'I don't know them. I've only met them a couple of times.'

'Was Jamie aware that you knew his parents?' This from Will again.

Allen stubbed his cigarette into a dish on top of the grand piano.

'He never asked, so probably not.' A note of irritation had crept into his voice. 'Look, I've explained . . . I met the Roscows twice, they're hardly friends. Is it important?'

'Did they know of your friendship with their son?'

Allen gave an exasperated sigh. 'I've no idea. You'll have to ask them.'

'You didn't mention your place in Cornwall to them?'

'No, yes . . . I don't know. Maybe. I don't exactly make a secret of the fact that I have a home down there.'

He took a breath and flashed them a forced smile. 'Now, gentlemen, if that's all, I have a room full of dinner guests and they will be thinking I have abandoned them.'

'Of course.' Sam smiled back. 'Please

apologize to your guests on our behalf. Thank you for your time, sir.'

Allen lifted an arm, still fixing Will and Sam with his practised smile, indicating the way out.

Sam spun round as he reached the door. 'I know you're busy, sir, but . . . hmm . . . I don't suppose we could impose on your time for just a few minutes more? I'd love to see where you work. My partner is such a fan of crime thrillers.' He ignored Will's attempt to hide his surprise and gave Allen an appealing look. 'She would be made up if I could describe where you write your books.'

'I don't write here. All my work is done in Cornwall. I thought you realized that.'

Sam gave a disappointed nod.

Allen relented. 'I tell you what. Why not pop along to see me there? I'll show you around the house.' He described the Karrek house Sam and Will had called at the previous day and the detective thanked him.

'Actually, why not bring your partner with you,' Allen said. 'What's her name?'

'Loveday.'

'Very well, bring Loveday round for drinks. Give me a ring when it's convenient.'

'Thank you. I will.'

Back in the car the detectives sat for a few minutes looking back at the house.

'You didn't ask him about the fogou?' Will said.

'He would have lied in his teeth, and it would have tipped him off about how much we already know about him. No, I'm keeping that one up my sleeve for the time being.'

Will gave Sam a curious look as he buckled up.

'He didn't like being asked about Jamie's folks, did he, boss?'

'No,' Sam said thoughtfully. 'He certainly didn't.'

Will's brow wrinkled as a new thought struck him.

'Could he have been passing on information about Jamie to his parents?'

'That's exactly what I was thinking,' Sam said, nodding towards the ignition key. 'Mr Allen has a lot more explaining

129

to do, and I think he knows it.'

They were on the M5 speeding towards Cornwall when Will said, 'that was a good ploy to get that invite from our author friend. I had no idea Loveday was such a fan of crime thrillers.'

Sam smiled. 'Neither does she, Will . . . not yet.'

*   *   *

It was after six when Loveday drove into Marazion. The streets were quiet but she knew that was only because the tourists would all be in the pubs and restaurants having their evening meal. They would be out soon enough, strolling along the front, taking yet more pictures of St Michael's Mount, making the most of what was left of the day to play with their children on the beach.

Cassie's big four by four and Adam's red hatchback were both in the drive, but there was no sign of Sam's Lexus. She parked the Clio by the kitchen door, grabbing her brown leather shoulder bag from the front passenger seat before letting herself into the cottage.

Her phone rang as she was slipping off her jacket and she rummaged in her bag for it. It was Sam.

'You didn't have plans for this evening, did you?'

'Other than pouring myself a large glass of ice-cold wine, then no. Why?' she asked warily. 'What are you up to, Sam?'

'Why should I be up to anything? You have such a suspicious mind, Loveday.' He sounded relaxed, chirpy even, and that could mean only one thing.

'We won't be finished here till late so I'll sleep at the cottage tonight. No point in coming in the wee small hours and waking you.'

Loveday knew he meant his cottage in Stithians, the one he once shared with his late and beautiful young wife, Tessa — the cottage he couldn't bring himself to sell.

She tried not to get angry. 'I don't mind you being late, really I don't.'

'But I do. You need your sleep, Loveday, and you've had precious little of that over the past few days.'

If she hadn't known Sam better she

would have thought it was an excuse
— but this was Sam — and he didn't lie.
She didn't tell him she would sleep better
if he was in bed beside her. Loveday still
found it difficult coming to terms with
why Sam kept on his cottage in Stithians.
She knew why, of course, it was his link to
the past . . . his link to Tessa, and he
didn't want to let go of that.

Just when she thought she'd got over
his still lingering devotion to his late wife,
it all came flooding back at moments like
this, followed by the inevitable guilt.

Tessa had been the victim of a drunk
driver, a man who was now dead himself.
It was all in the past. She knew how
devastated Sam had been at the time, but
that was years ago, and he was with her
now.

'Is everything all right, Loveday? You
sound funny.'

'What?' She'd almost forgotten she was
still holding the phone. 'Eh, no, everything's fine. I agree, it makes sense to
sleep at Stithians if you're going to be
really late.'

'Will and I are in London interviewing

a witness. Could be the early hours before we're back in Cornwall. I'll ring later to update you.'

London! That took her by surprise.

'You certainly get around, Inspector. Who's the witness?'

'No one you know.'

'Is that code for mind my own business?'

Sam laughed. 'Would there be any point in my telling you that?'

'No.' She could imagine his slow grin as he shook his head at the phone.

'You're sounding better,' he said, the tease still in his voice.

'I'm fine, Sam, really. Don't worry about me. You drive carefully down there.'

'I always drive carefully, not so sure about Will though. It's a pool car we've got, so he's been doing the honours. Oh . . . I nearly forgot. Can you do me a favour and take a look at that book I brought back last night. It's a detective paperback. I'd be interested to know what you think about it.'

Loveday screwed up her nose. 'What's so important about the book, Sam?'

'Nothing. You don't have to look at it if you have other stuff to do. It's not that important.'

But Loveday's antenna was already working, as he knew it would.

She sighed. 'Where do I find this book?'

It was where he'd left it on his bedside table. She hadn't noticed it when she'd left that morning. Now she was examining it, turning it over in her hands. The cover was dark and moody; a body sprawled over glistening wet cobbles in a grim backstreet, a slash of crimson blood seeping from the victim's throat. There was a brief synopsis on the back cover, together with a professionally posed picture of the author, Desmond Height — the man, according to Maya, that no one in Karrek had a good word for.

She'd never read any of his books, and if this was an example she doubted if she would be investing in any of his future work.

A sudden twang of hunger reminded her she'd hardly eaten that day and she dropped the book on the coffee table in the cottage's tiny sitting room as she went into the kitchen to check what was in the fridge.

There wasn't a great choice. Eggs, cheese, pickle, half of a sorry-looking lettuce and some shrunken mushrooms. She frowned at the depleted shelves. Why hadn't she done a food shop?

Loveday hated supermarket shopping at the best of times, but it seemed even worse in the evening. Staff who had been on their feet all day were looking irritated, and the store had none of its busy daytime buzz.

She pushed her trolley around the aisles in double quick time, tossing in cereal, and packs of meat, vegetables, salads, bread, milk and coffee. Her favourite Chardonnay was on offer so she snatched up three bottles.

By the time she got back to the cottage, Marazion had come alive again. Everyone was enjoying the fine May weather, couples strolled arm in arm along the front and the car parks were still busy.

Half an hour later, the shopping had been unpacked, the fridge and larder cupboard stocked up again, and a salmon steak, drizzled in olive oil and sprinkled with seasoning, was in foil and baking in the oven. Loveday had washed half the contents of a bag of salad and poured herself a large glass of wine. She had been about to collapse onto a kitchen chair when she remembered Walter Allen's book.

She went through to the sitting room and picked it up, flicking through the pages as she took it to the kitchen table. And then she stopped, her eyes widening as she stared at the open page. She knew now why Sam had asked her to read it.

The hand penned inscription to Jamie had been done with a flourish. Maya had mentioned Jamie was one of the few people who spoke to Walter Allen, but she hadn't got the impression they were friends. So why had the writer given him a signed copy of his novel? Maybe he liked to mix with creative people, which would explain how he got to know Ben. But did he also mix with writers? Why not? She wished she'd known about this earlier. She could have asked Maya more about it.

The pinging of the oven timer interrupted her thoughts. She'd forgotten about the salmon. She ate her meal with the dog-eared paperback propped up in front of her.

The violence started on page one as the story opened with a brutal murder, described in colourful language by the narrator detective. Loveday skim read it to chapter five, by which time body number one had been joined by two more, all having suffered equally gruesome ends. She sighed. Did people really write this stuff?

She got up and poured herself another Chardonnay before opening her laptop. A Google check on the Desmond Height name led her to the writer's Amazon author page, and his impressive catalogue of books. Loveday shook her head; her eyes scrolling down the list. The man had produced about twenty of them, all apparently in the same garish, salacious form — and all of them boasting high numbers of great reader reviews.

She sat back, sighing. Was she missing something? Either she had no taste in current commercial crime fiction, or she was in the wrong business.

She glanced across to her mobile phone. She was itching to ring Sam and ask why this book interested him. The fact that the author had given it to Jamie didn't even necessarily mean the two were friends. Perhaps he hadn't given the book away. Jamie could have bought it at one of the author's book signing events and asked him to sign it in this particular way.

She picked it up again. By the state of it, Jamie must have read it over and over again. Loveday opened the back cover. Someone had been scribbling on it. The faded words had been written in pencil and were now hardly even decipherable.

She held it away from her, squinting at the writing. The last line seemed to be a bit clearer than the rest. It looked like — 'Pathetic . . . should be banned under the trade description act. This is not any kind of literature!'

'Hmm,' she muttered to herself. 'Well

not everybody loved Mr Height's work.' Flicking through the pages and reading odd ones at random it appeared that the story continued in the same vein. The body count had risen, along with the lathering of crude four letter words. Loveday's sympathies were with the scribbler at the back. It was a terrible book!

\* \* \*

It was after midnight when Sam drove into Stithians and turned into his drive. He sat for a moment staring at the small stone outhouse illuminated in his headlights. Tessa's workshop. All her jewellery-making equipment was still in there. Everything exactly as Tessa had left it on that last day. A shiver ran through him. It was years since she had died — killed at the hands of a drunk driver.

He'd been so bitter. Getting even with the man had been the thing that had kept him going all through those early years following her death.

His hatred of the man never went away,

not even after he met Loveday. He had to have his revenge — for Tessa's sake. He wouldn't have killed Brian Penrose, just roughed him up a bit. He could still remember standing outside Exeter Prison waiting for the man on the day he was released. In Sam's mind he was back there now, eyes fixed on the blue prison door as it opened and Penrose stepped out onto the cobbles.

He still remembered his horror as the car roared in from nowhere and slammed into the man. He'd died instantly. It hadn't made Sam feel any better.

He turned the car's ignition key and the lights died. For a few more minutes he sat there, staring into the darkness. The street lamps cast a shadow over his cottage. He didn't really know why he hadn't sold the place. He knew that was what Loveday wanted. Maybe she was right. Maybe it was time he let go of the past.

An image of his first wife, Victoria, drifted into his mind, but she was still very much alive in Plymouth with their children, Jack and Maddie. He didn't see nearly enough of them, but he hadn't lost them. And now he had Loveday in his life as well. There was much to be thankful for.

# 11

Moving to the new station hadn't provided Sam with the bigger office he'd been hoping for, but he'd grudgingly admitted that the current venue at the top end of Truro, near the courts, made better sense than being stuck on a main road on the edge of town where they were constantly having to negotiate one of the city's busiest roundabouts.

The actual transfer had been a nightmare and there were still files he doubted he would ever see again, but he and his colleagues were here now and everyone seemed to be getting used to their new surroundings.

Sam moved away from the window and stared thoughtfully at the post mortem report that lay open on his desk.

Jamie had died from being struck on the head twice with a blunt object. His skull was caved in, causing a bleed to the brain.

Sam sighed. Poor Jamie. Even if he had survived the attack it was likely he would have been left with severe brain damage.

A forensic examination of the area where the body had been found concluded that the attack had happened inside the fogou. Sam flipped that file open as well and ran his eyes over the contents.

Now that they knew Jamie had died inside the cave they had to work out what he was doing there. Had he gone willingly to the fogou with his killer, or had they met by arrangement? And why there? According to Clem Tangye Walter Allen knew all about the place, and he was definitely worth having a closer look at.

Maya was the only other person that he knew for sure had been interested in the fogou. He hadn't discounted her from the investigation. She had certainly appeared very upset when they told her Jamie's body had been identified, but then she could be a brilliant actress.

He closed the files and was about to summons his team to the morning briefing when his phone rang.

'Superintendent Bolger would like to see you in his office. Now, please,' the crisp voice of his superior officer's secretary, Adele Traves, instructed.

Sam sighed. He wasn't in the mood for a lecture. The investigation was hardly moving on at all. And now he would have to explain why.

He made his way to the top floor, using the stairs rather than the lift and paused to take a deep breath before going in to the big man's office.

Adele Traves glanced up at him over the top of her spectacles and nodded towards the senior officer's door. 'Super-intendent Bolger is waiting for you. Please go in.'

Sam did. The man behind the desk did not greet him with a smile.

'The top brass is breathing down my neck, so I'm breathing down yours,' he growled at Sam. 'We need to get this case moving, DI Kitto.'

Sam hadn't needed reminding how many days had passed since they'd found Jamie's body

He cleared his throat ready to explain

that he knew all that, but the senior officer raised a hand to stop him.

'Unless you're about to tell me you've caught our murderer, and he's banged up in the cells at this very minute, then don't say anything.'

Sam's mouth pressed into a hard line. He was struggling to keep his temper in the face of the man's rudeness.

Superintendent Bolger got to his feet and began pacing of the room. And then he'd stopped, perching his large bottom on the edge of his desk, looming over Sam. It was a deliberately intimidating pose. The man was actually trying to bully him. Sam could feel his temper rising, his fists going into tight balls. It took all of his control not to rise to this bait.

He took a breath and once again attempted to give a quick appraisal of the investigation, but the man wasn't listening. He only wanted results.

Sam thought about disclosing the fact that he and Loveday would be taking up Walter Allen's invitation to visit his house in Karrek, but then decided against it. If nothing came of it he might end up with egg on his face, and that was not something he would relish.

The big man was thumping his desk with his fist. 'We need to be much more pro-active, Detective Inspector Kitto.' His voice rose again as he pushed his face closer to Sam's to emphasize his point. 'Don't let that team of yours sit on their fat arses. Get them out there. We need results!'

Sam's fists were still balled as he'd stormed away from Bolger's office. He'd been swallowing hard, trying to hold on to his temper. Had the man thought he was an idiot? Sitting on their fat arses was not a luxury his team enjoyed. That was more in the superintendent's domain.

He was still fuming when he strode back into the CID room and called his team to the briefing. He took a few minutes in his office before joining them. Bolger was a nasty creature, but he had a point. Things needed stirring up. They had to move this investigation on.

The CID team was gathered around the big oval table in the station's conference room when Sam joined them. He glanced up as he passed the wall of photographs. The gruesome collection from the scene showing Jamie's body in situ was a grim reminder that they were no closer to solving this murder than they'd been at the start. Well, no, that wasn't true. Walter Allen definitely knew more than he was saying. He was looking forward to taking up the man's invitation to call in on him at his house in Karrek. He'd used Loveday to angle for that invitation. She might not appreciate that but he knew she would find the challenge irresistible.

Sam studied the faces on the wall. Jamie, Maya, Walter Allen, Clem Tangye, even the Badger Inn was up there. DC Fox hadn't wasted her time when Sam sent her to interview potential witnesses. And then he frowned. What was Ben Poldavy's photograph doing on the wall? He'd given Amanda no instructions to include him. The young detective had acted on her own initiative. Under different circumstances he would have praised her . . . but Ben? Why hadn't he been told? And Amanda hadn't produced her witness statement. He'd seen no record of her interview with Ben. He wasn't happy!

He pulled a blank expression. Whatever his personal feelings, this was a murder investigation and they could leave no stone unturned. Ben's photo would soon come down from the Murder Wall, as they called it. They would quickly rule him out of the investigation. He was sure of it. But the anger inside him was growing. He needed to focus. He scanned the faces around the table, stopping when he reached Amanda.

'OK, DC Fox, tell us what you know.'

Amanda stood up, securing a loose pin in the scrunched up bun she had pulled her wiry red hair into, as she crossed to the Murder Wall and pointed to Ben's picture.

'Ben Poldavy, artist, was a friend of Jamie's. They met six months ago at one of Poldavy's exhibitions in Penzance. Jamie showed an interest in his work and Ben invited him back to his cottage in Polmarth to see more of his paintings.'

DC Malcolm Carter lifted his head from his notebook. 'So are we saying Poldavy's a suspect then?'

Amanda shot a glance to Sam, but his expression revealed nothing of what was going on in his head. 'What do you think, DC Fox?' he said. 'Is Mr Poldavy a suspect?'

Amanda frowned and turned back to Ben's picture. 'Not sure,' she said slowly. 'But he's interesting. For a start he knew about the fogou — '

Sam's head snapped up. He hadn't known that, but then Ben would have had no reason to mention it, not unless he had been directly asked.

He said, 'How did he know about it?'

'Apparently he makes it his business to familiarize himself with all the oddities in his area — standing stones, ancient burial chambers, that kind of thing. He paints them.'

'Are you saying he's actually painted our fogou?' Sam asked.

'Yes. I've seen it,' Amanda said. 'And he's not a bad artist.'

'Has he ever been there with our

victim?' Sam wanted to know.

Amanda shrugged. 'He said not.' She paused. 'But the thing is . . . Jamie saw the painting and was showing a great interest in it.'

Everyone waited for her to continue, but she shrugged again. 'That's it. I thought Poldavy was interesting. I'm sure he has more to tell us. It might be helpful if I go back there with you today.' She looked at Sam.

He considered it for a second, easing himself off the edge of the table he had perched on and moving to the front of the room. 'No, it's fine. You have a witness statement to write.'

Amanda blushed. 'Sorry, sir. It was late when I got back to the station last night. My witness statement's almost finished . . . I . . . '

Sam's slow shake of the head cut her off. He was standing in front of the Murder Wall looking around the dozen faces. 'In future, witness statements will be on my desk *before* you go home, and that means all of you. Is that clear?'

They all nodded. It wasn't often Sam read the riot act to his team, but every now and again they need a reminder that this was a murder investigation. He had no intention of allowing sloppy police work to damage his case.

He turned to Will, clearing his throat. 'Any more news on our murder weapon?'

Will shook his head. 'None. Every inch of the site was searched and it wasn't there. What do we know about it?'

'Only that it's some kind of blunt object,' Sam said. 'It could be anything from a tree branch to a hammer, or it could be one of those big stones lying around the site.'

'Well, if it wasn't a stone then the killer could have taken the weapon with him,' Amanda said.

'Or her,' Sam corrected, and had the satisfaction of seeing the detective blush again. 'But you're probably right, which means it could be anywhere now.'

Even if they found the killer they might never find the weapon.

One by one the officers described the leads they were following. None of them sounded like they would be particularly fruitful.

'What about our victim's parents, DC Carter? Have you managed to track them down yet?'

'I haven't actually spoken to them,' Malcolm said, not hiding the apologetic tone in his voice. 'They were on a cruise ship somewhere out in the Caribbean. But I got a message through to the ship and they were supposed to be flying home some time during the night.'

Sam tutted. He should have dealt with this himself. 'Do they actually know their son is dead?'

'Yes, sir, it was done through the ship's captain.'

'Right, find out what flight they're on and make sure someone contacts them. I'll drive to London later today and speak to them myself.'

Malcolm Carter nodded. 'Yes, sir.'

'We also need to have another word with Ben Poldavy.'

Amanda looked up expectantly.

'I'll go, sir.'

'No, I want to interview him myself.'

He raised an eyebrow, ignoring Amanda's scowl. 'Does anyone else have anything to add?'

One after the other they shook their heads.

'Well, we've all got plenty of work to do, let's get on with it,' Sam said, collecting his files and heading back to his office. When he got there he dropped into his chair. Bolger was right, the case was drifting and it was Sam's fault. He was the senior investigating officer. He was supposed to be in charge and they were making no progress. The time had come to tighten up the whole investigation.

Amanda looked up as Sam reappeared from his office and beckoned Will to follow him. She had expected praise for her previous day's work, and for what she had discovered from her interview with the artist, Ben Poldavy, but all her boss had been interested in at the morning briefing was that blessed witness statement.

She looked away, trying to appear busy as Sam and Will walked past her, heading for the door. She knew they were going back to re-interview Ben Poldavy.

She waited until they were almost out of the room before giving Sam's back a mutinous glare. He was always favouring Will Tregellis over her. If he was such a great detective how come he was still only a DS? She'd be a chief inspector by the time she reached thirty.

She waited until the pair had cleared the CID suite before going to the window to catch sight of them as they commandeered a car from the pool of police vehicles.

She'd tried to duck out of sight as Sam glanced up, but she hadn't been quick enough. He'd spotted her. Even at this distance he could see the fury on her face. He knew that she had wanted, and had no doubt expected to be the one who went with him to interview Ben Poldavy again. Maybe she was right, but this was not the day to exhibit such pettiness. Besides, Sam had the impression that Amanda was already prejudiced against Ben.

He instructed Will to drive as he got

into the passenger seat. There was thinking to be done. Sam's head pounded as they picked their way through the narrow congested streets of Truro. Question after question chased around in his mind, like an express train rushing through a tunnel, except nothing came out at the other end. Maybe Ben would have some answers for them. He certainly hoped so.

They took the A30, heading out towards Land's End. Sam was aware of the sidelong glances from his colleague, but Will knew better than to speak.

Sam was working out the best approach for this interview. He couldn't let the fact that Ben was a friend influence him. If there was any doubt to clear up then he was the one who would do it. He didn't want to alienate Ben, but he *did* want to see that painting of the fogou Amanda had talked about.

There was not another vehicle in sight as Will turned down the lane that led to Ben and Keri's cottage. His old Land Rover was parked out front, but there was no sign of Ben. Sam rattled the knocker but there was no response. He had been about to send Will round to the back of the cottage to check when he spotted Ben strolling towards them, a plastic carrier bag in his hand.

He frowned, not sure whether to smile a welcome to not. He held up the bag. 'Bread and milk.'

Sam nodded. 'We need a quick word, Ben. D'you mind?'

Ben shrugged, but the frown stayed on his face. 'I'm getting a lot of visits from the police these days.' He paused, front door key in his hand. 'I take it this *is* a police visit, Sam?'

Sam swallowed. 'We think you might be able to help us, Ben.'

'You'd better come in then.' Ben unlocked the cottage door and the two detectives followed him into the kitchen, where Ben plonked his shopping on the table and turned to face them.

'You said I could help. How?'

'You had a visit from DC Fox yesterday.'

Ben's eyes flashed. 'So that's it. She thinks I'm guilty of something, doesn't she?' He met Sam's calm stare. 'I've done nothing wrong. It was me who asked you to check up on Jamie in the first place.'

Sam felt Will's sharp look, but the man was too much of a professional to show surprise. The explanations could wait.

'DC Fox said you knew about the fogou where we . . . where Jamie's body was found.'

Ben waited a beat, trying to weigh up any implication in the question.

'I know the place, yes,' he said slowly, removing the bread and milk from the plastic carrier bag. 'I've painted it.'

'What can you tell us about it?'

Ben shrugged, putting the bread into a large white chipped enamel bread bin. 'It's old . . . mysterious. No one is quite sure what it was built for.'

He turned to put the milk in the fridge. 'Sorry, I'm being a poor host. Keri would be ticking me off for that. Can I get you a coffee?'

They both shook their heads.

'Beer then?' Ben said.

Will's hopeful look extracted a relenting smile from Sam. He nodded towards the fridge. 'A beer would be great. Thanks, Ben.'

The acceptance wasn't only to appease his sergeant. Things got more relaxed when you shared a drink with someone. People allowed their guard to fall, not that Sam was trying to catch Ben out.

They sipped their beer from the cans, leaning against the worktops in the kitchen.

'You were telling us about the fogou,' Sam reminded him. 'How did you know about it?'

'Everyone around here knows about it. It's part of the landscape, but these old Cornish things interest me.' A pause. 'Like I said, I've painted it . . . but then you will already know that.'

Sam ignored the comment.

'Any chance of you showing us that painting, Ben?'

Ben took another swig of his beer and put the can on the worktop.

'You'd better come through to my studio.' He led them through the cottage and out the back door. A sharp wind was buffeting the tangy smell of salt straight at them.

Will gasped at the view, his eyes skimming over the spectacular panoramic seascape. 'You're not exactly short of subject matter, here,' he said.

Ben followed his gaze, narrowing his eyes against the breeze. 'We're very lucky. My paintings are in here.'

He led them to a small stone outhouse at the far side of the unkempt wild garden.

Sam's nose wrinkled as the pungent smell of linseed oil hit them as soon as they entered the building. It wasn't unpleasant.

Ben rifled through a stack of canvasses and selected one from the back.

'I think this is what you're interested in.' He handed the painting to Sam.

Will's eyebrows rose in approval. 'It's exactly what it looks like. How'd you manage that?'

'Did you show this to Jamie?' Sam asked.

'He found it himself.'

The two detectives looked at him.

'Jamie asked if he could see my work. I told him he was welcome to have a rummage around. The only one he asked questions about was the fogou.' A smile crossed his face as he remembered. 'He was fascinated by it . . . wanted to know more.'

'Did he explain why he was so interested in the fogou?' Will asked.

'Jamie's girlfriend is affiliated to a museum in Helston. I mean she's not on the permanent staff, more like an archaeologist in residence or something like that. She writes information sheets on ancient relics. He told me that.'

'Did he say anything about visiting the fogou?' Sam cut in.

'Not as such,' Ben said, 'but he asked for directions to find it, so I assumed he was planning to go there.'

'But he never actually told you he had been there?' Sam said.

'No.' Ben looked from one to the other. 'Is any of this helping?'

Sam wasn't sure, but he smiled. 'It helps to fit in another part of the puzzle.'

Ben had taken the painting back from Will and was holding it at arm's length, studying it.

'It's odd though,' he said slowly. 'Jamie must have seen this painting at my exhibition.' He looked up. 'That's how we met . . . when he came to my exhibition in Penzance. Did I mention that?'

Sam nodded. 'You said it was odd. What was odd?'

'Only that Jamie hadn't particularly mentioned the painting then, if at all. And yet when he saw it here he was absolutely fascinated.'

A thought stuck Sam, but it didn't make any sense.

He frowned. 'When Jamie came here asking to see more of your work.' He paused, trying to put his thoughts in some kind of order. 'Did you get the impression that he had come specifically to see that painting?'

Ben looked back at his canvas and tilted his head at it, considering. 'Now that you mention it, well, yes. I suppose I did.'

He glanced up at the officers. 'Do you

161

think it means something?'

Sam's lips pursed. 'I wish I knew, Ben.'

But Sam's feelings were stronger than that. If Jamie had come to Ben's cottage with the particular intention of studying the painting of the fogou then it almost certainly did mean something.

By the time they left, Sam was more certain than ever that Ben had nothing to do with Jamie's murder.

'Let's find a cup of coffee,' he said as he and Will got back into the pool car. 'We have some thinking to do.'

# 12

Sam's mobile rang as he and Will went in search of a cafe. It was DC Fox. 'Amanda. What's up?'

'The Roscows are here.'

'What?'

'The Roscows. Jamie Roscow's parents. They're here, boss. And they're asking for you.'

Sam sighed. 'Right. Where exactly are they?'

'I've put them in your office. They're not happy.'

Why would they be happy? They'd lost their son.

'I'm depending on you to keep them occupied, Amanda. Don't leave them alone. Take them to the canteen or something. Just keep them calm until we get there. Can you do that?'

There was a pause and he could hear Amanda drawing in her breath.

'This is important. Do you understand

that?' He spoke more sharply than he had intended. Why could she not simply be nice to these parents? Couldn't she see what they must be going through?

He could hear her clearing her throat at the other end of the phone.

'Of course, sir,' she said stiffly. 'I'll look after them for you.'

Sam cringed at the words. DC Amanda Fox would have to change her patronizing attitude if she wanted to stay in his team.

'I'm not asking you to do me a favour, Amanda,' he said, his voice rising. 'I'm telling you to look after the Roscows because it's your job. Am I getting through?'

He knew Will was looking at him, but this young officer was so exasperating.

'Eh . . . yes, of course, boss.' She hesitated. 'I'll look after them.'

'We'll be back at the nick in an hour,' Sam said curtly. 'We'll see you then.'

It was fifty minutes later when Sam and Will walked into the CID room. Amanda leapt to her feet, phone at her ear. She muttered something into the mouthpiece and slid her eyes in the direction of Sam's small office.

He shot her a frown. Why hadn't she stayed with them like he'd told her to do? What was wrong with her today?

'Come with me, Will,' he instructed, striding into his office.

His nose twitched as the strong smell of expensive perfume hit him. Sarah Roscow's head jerked up when they came into the room. She didn't wait for introductions.

'At last! You *do* know we have been waiting here for the past two hours.'

'I'm sorry,' Sam started, including the man standing at the window in his remarks, 'DS Tregellis and I were unavoidably detained. If we'd known you were arriving this morning we could have arranged things differently.'

The woman's bright red lips pressed themselves into a disgruntled hard line and her angry blue eyes glared at Sam from under spikey black lashes.

'We got here as fast as we could, Inspector,' Charles Roscow said, coming forward to take the hand Sam offered.

'We were in the Caribbean when we got the news.' His tanned brow furrowed. 'I don't suppose there could be any mistake. I mean it *is* Jamie?'

Sam gave a serious nod. 'Jamie's body has been identified by one of his friends.'

Sarah Roscow rose from her chair, brushed down the pleated pink skirt that matched her jacket and drew herself up to her 5ft 4. 'We'd like to see our son now, Inspector,' she said briskly.

Sam gave Will the nod to check with the mortuary and turned back to Jamie's parents as he left the room.

'Your son's body is at the hospital. We'll take you there.'

He watched them in the driving mirror as he negotiated his Lexus through the busy city streets. Mrs Roscow's cold bright eyes stared out at the passing traffic. Her husband's expression was composed, but Sam could see his control was forced. The man was obviously in pain.

The questions Sam needed to ask the couple could wait. Escorting parents to view the body of their dead child was not a task he relished.

Charles Roscow maintained his composure as the white-coated mortuary attendant removed the sheet from Jamie's face, but his wife let out a cry and buried her face in her hands. Charles attempted to put his arm around her shoulders, but she pulled back, shrugging it off.

'This is all your fault. You drove Jamie to this.' She spat out the words, her voice rising. 'You killed our son!'

Sam and Will shot forward, grabbing her as she launched herself at her husband, fists flying.

The startled attendant stepped back.

'He did it!' The woman stabbed a finger at her husband. 'This is all his fault!'

'Will, can you ring the station for a car to take Mr Roscow back . . . and go with him.' He glanced at Mrs Roscow's enraged face. 'We'll see you there.'

Will nodded, ushering the man out of the mortuary. Sam gave them a minute before putting a hand on Mrs Roscow's back and steering her in the direction of the hospital canteen.

The lunchtime rush was over and Sam found a quiet table on the far side of the room. Sarah's earlier outburst seemed to have drained her energy and she offered no objection. She sank onto a plastic chair, dropping her cream leather handbag on the floor.

Sam fetched them two mugs of strong sweet tea and sat down opposite.

Sarah cupped her hands around the mug and lifted it to her mouth. She reminded Sam of a child, not quite sure how she should behave. The liquid was scalding, but she still sipped it, and then sat back, her shoulders sagging. She looked up at Sam; all signs of the earlier fire had vanished. It was a defeated woman who sat in front of him now.

He put the wooden stirring spatula into his mug and gave the liquid a swirl.

'This must be unbelievably difficult for you. I'm so sorry.'

She blinked, not answering.

They sipped their tea in silence for a while, Sam happy to give the woman time to recover from her violent outburst.

And then she said, 'You'll want to

know what that behaviour just now was all about. So would I.' She sounded defeated. 'Poor Charles. He didn't deserve that. I wanted to lash out, and he was there. I'll apologize later.'

'Grief affects people in different ways,' Sam said gently. 'Your husband will understand.'

Sarah reached down for her bag, snapped it open and drew out a wad of tissues. She pulled a couple from the top, dabbed them at her eyes and gave a shuddering sigh.

'Jamie was my baby. I wanted him to have the best . . . best school, best friends, and best career. But it wasn't what Jamie wanted. I used to get so angry with him. He was throwing his life away and he didn't realize it.' Her voice trembled. 'And now he's gone!'

Her fist tightened around the scrunch of tissues, but there were no more tears.

The carefully made up face took on its hard expression again.

'We gave Jamie everything, you know, and he threw it all back in our faces.'

The flint blue eyes narrowed. 'He ran

away from school. Charlton Public School. It is the best school in the country, but it wasn't good enough for Jamie. He ran away.' Her shoulders gave a helpless shrug. 'He could have worked alongside us running the business, but no, that wasn't good enough for Jamie either.' She shook her head. 'Always such an ungrateful boy.'

Sam studied her face. He was beginning to understand why Jamie chose to remove himself from this controlling mother. He didn't doubt she loved her son, her reaction when she saw his body proved that. But it was all on her terms. Poor Jamie must have felt he was being smothered in this family. He wondered what part Charles Roscow had played in it all.

'We even introduced him to nice girls, but none of them ever suited him. He wasn't even interested in trying. And I had begun to wonder if he was gay.'

'Would that have been a problem?' Sam asked.

'Oh, I don't know. These people seem to be accepted in society now. Not that it matters. We know Jamie wasn't gay.'

'How do you know?'

'The string of hippy girlfriends for a start. He had no taste. He liked to go off and 'do his own thing' as he was so fond of saying, but we always found him. He always returned home.'

She looked up at him. 'I want to see where Jamie lived. Can you take me there?'

The request took Sam by surprise, but the woman had every right to ask. He wondered what Maya would have to say about it. He needed to ring her.

'Just let me make a call,' he said, stepping away from the table. He could feel her eyes on him as he punched out Maya's number. She answered at once. He heard her sharp intake of breath when he told her that Jamie's mother had requested to visit his boat.

'Is that OK?' he asked.

'Do I need to be here?' Maya said.

'That's up to you, but as you were one of Jamie's close friends I imagine Mrs Roscow would like to meet you.'

Her agreement to meet them on the

boat was given grudgingly. He sensed how nervous she was.

'Should we collect your husband on the way, Mrs Roscow?' Sam asked as he walked with her out of the hospital. 'Perhaps he would also like to see where your son lived.'

The woman shook her head. 'He can go later if he wishes, let's do this now.'

She didn't utter another word until they drove into Karrek, but he could sense her body stiffening as the creek came into view.

'Is that it?' she asked quietly, nodding towards the *April Rose*.

Sam confirmed that it was.

'Who is the young woman I can see on the deck?'

'Maya Brookes. She was a friend of Jamie's. She's looking after the boat.'

Sam parked close to the pub and they walked along the bank together. Maya offered Mrs Roscow her hand and introduced herself as the woman climbed on board.

Sam followed them down into the saloon and saw Jamie's mother wrinkle her nose in distaste as she looked around the galley. 'This is where my son lived?' She was clearly not impressed.

Maya cleared her throat. 'Jamie loved this boat. He and Scobey took great pride in restoring it.'

Mrs Roscow met her eyes. 'Scobey?'

'A friend of ours who had been helping Jamie with the boat.'

'Is he here, this Scobey?'

'I'm Scobey,' the voice behind them said.

They all wheeled round. None of them had heard the man come on board.

He was staring at Mrs Roscow.

She blinked uncomfortably under his scrutiny. 'You knew my son?' she said.

Tom Scobey's expression was inscrutable, but Sam saw his eyes narrow behind the spectacles. He continued to stare at the woman.

She frowned. 'Have we met?' she asked.

'You don't know me,' Scobey said. 'We are strangers to each other. It was Jamie I knew.'

Sarah Roscow faced him with an unblinking stare. 'Tell me about him.

173

What was so special about this broken-down old boat that he preferred it to his home with us in London?'

Tom Scobey met her eyes, and Sam thought he saw the woman flinch. 'The *April Rose* was Jamie's home,' he said. 'He hated London. He hated living with you. You didn't know your son at all.'

Sarah Roscow's hand went to her throat and anger flamed in the piercing blue eyes.

Sam waited for the torrent of abuse he was sure she would rain down on Tom Scobey. But Sarah took a shuddering breath, looked away, and turned to stumble up the steps and off the boat.

Maya spun round to Scobey in surprise. 'Why were you so horrible to Jamie's mother?'

'She was never a mother to Jamie,' Scobey threw back, his voice full of anger. He stepped smartly out of the saloon leaving Sam and Maya to stare after him.

'Wait here,' Sam instructed, as he sprinted up the steps after him. But he stopped on the deck. Scobey had caught up with Sarah Roscow and the two were talking quietly. Sam could see she was crying. He should have intervened. Scobey's behaviour had been outrageous. However good or bad a mother she'd been they couldn't let that be the issue now.

Maya came up behind him. 'Is Mrs Roscow OK? I don't know what got into Scobey.'

Neither did Sam, but he would make it his business to find out. After he took Mrs Roscow to her hotel he would come back to speak to this man. He had some explaining to do.

By the time Sam made it up onto the bank, Scobey had turned, disappearing up the path through the trees. Mrs Roscow was standing alone, dabbing her eyes with a tissue when Sam reached her.

'Are you all right?'

She gave a gulping swallow and nodded. 'I'm fine. It's just seeing all this that makes me emotional.'

Sam thought it more likely that it was Tom Scobey's harsh words that had made the woman weep.

'I'll take you back to your husband,' he

said gently, taking her arm and leading her to his car.

The drive back to Truro was completed in virtual silence, but the woman did seem to have recovered from her distress and stared moodily out at the busy road.

A thought struck Sam as they joined the city traffic. 'Mrs Roscow, did you know your son was in Cornwall?'

Sarah gave him an incredulous look. 'Of course we did. We always knew where Jamie was. Oh, he tried to cover his tracks more than ever this time, but he could never fool us.'

'How did you find out Jamie was in Cornwall?' He was expecting to hear that the couple had hired a private detective.

'Walter, of course,' she said. 'He's been keeping an eye on Jamie for us.' She paused, her bottom lip trembling. '*Had* been keeping an eye on Jamie.'

Sam blinked. 'I didn't realize you knew Walter Allen.'

'Of course we do. Walter and Elizabeth are on our dinner party list.'

Sam's eyebrows came together in a frown. So Walter Allen had lied to them.

Now why would he do that? Here was another man with explaining to do. Suddenly Sam was looking forward to visiting the writer at his house in Karrek.

# 13

'There's someone to see you in reception,' Keri said.

Loveday's fingers were flying over her keyboard.

'Who is it?' she asked without looking up.

'Some woman. She wouldn't give her name.'

Loveday wasn't sure what to expect as she walked into the magazine's small reception area, but it certainly wasn't the slight girl who looked up with an embarrassed smile when she saw her.

Loveday took in the short denim jacket, the yellow flowery cotton dress, and the strappy gladiator-type sandals. Her fringed tapestry shoulder bag was slung horizontally across her front.

'Maya!'

The young woman looked flustered. 'I didn't want to interrupt you.'

'You're not,' Loveday assured. 'It's

lovely to see you. Why don't we go out and grab a coffee?'

She ushered Maya out of the tiny marbled floor reception and into busy Lemon Street. The town centre was buzzing with activity as they made their way through the crowds of shoppers, and round the corner into Boscawen Street and the bookshop.

Upstairs in the coffee shop they found a corner table. Loveday waited until they had steaming mugs of coffee in front of them before starting.

'So how are you, Maya?' She fixed her attention on the girl's earnest green eyes.

'Oh, you know . . . bearing up.'

'Really?'

Maya stirred her coffee, avoiding Loveday's gaze. 'Well . . . '

Loveday reached across the table and touched the girl's arm. 'No one is expecting you to be Superwoman. I'm sure all your friends want you to look after yourself.'

Maya's eyes filled with tears, and she made a frustrated swipe at them. 'I didn't come here for sympathy. That's the last thing I need, but I want your help, Loveday.'

'Of course. Whatever I can do.'

'I think I know who killed Jamie.'

Loveday blinked, not sure she had heard right. 'Have you been to the police?'

'I don't have any proof. How can I take it to the police? They would laugh at me. That's why I've come to you. I *had* to tell someone.'

'OK,' Loveday said slowly, 'so tell me.'

Maya took a long steadying breath, and then she said, 'He'd been behaving funny around Jamie for months, acting like he was his best friend. He was always hanging around and then appearing out of the blue on the boat. He even tried to foist one of his horrible books on Jamie.' Her voice hesitated. 'And he'd been asking questions about him behind his back.'

Loveday leaned forward. 'Are you talking about Walter Allen?'

'Yes, that's who I mean.'

'I'm not sure what you've just said amounts to enough evidence of murder,' Loveday said.

'Well, I said I didn't have any proof, but the more I think about it the more suspicious I become. The man was definitely up to something.'

Loveday lifted her cup and took a sip of the hot coffee. She was trying to imagine what Sam would make of this.

'I don't know this man, Maya, so I've got no idea what he's normally like. Maybe he really was trying to be friendly. It could all be perfectly innocent.'

'What do you think I should do?'

'Do nothing,' Loveday said. 'I'll mention your concerns to my policeman friend. He might want to come and see you again.'

'Thank you, Loveday. I appreciate that. I suppose I should have mentioned it when he brought Jamie's mother the boat yesterday.'

Loveday looked up. 'DI Kitto brought Mrs Roscow to the *April Rose*?' She felt a jab of annoyance that she hadn't known that. But then why should she? Sam didn't need to confide his every move to her.

'And that's the other thing I wanted to

talk to you about. Scobey came on board and was really nasty to the woman.' She looked away. 'It was so embarrassing.'

Loveday had only met the man briefly, but his distress at Jamie's murder had been obvious, even through that stone façade he had built around himself. But she wouldn't have expected him to launch a verbal attack on Jamie's mother.

But Maya was frowning.

Loveday met her eyes. 'You must try to stop worrying. We'll get this cleared up. I promise.'

Maya shook her head. 'It's not only that,' she said, her green eyes clouding over with concern.

Loveday waited.

The young woman dragged her gaze away from the far side of the room and drew in her breath.

'Scobey's disappeared!'

Loveday was trying to picture the man — blue denim shirt, shabby jeans and dark leather waistcoat, greying hair tied back in a stubby ponytail. She recalled thinking he reminded her of an ageing hippy.

Even though the interior of the narrowboat had been tiny and there were four of them in there, Scobey had managed to stay in the background. In fact she couldn't remember a single thing he had said. It was the pale grey eyes that gave him away. The shadow of grief there was unmistakeable.

The focus then had been on Maya. Loveday had got the impression that if the man had known she and Sam would be turning up he would have stayed out of the way altogether.

She lifted her cup and took a sip of the strong black coffee. 'When did you last see him?'

'About five o'clock yesterday. He came back after your policeman friend took Jamie's mother away. He said he wanted to apologize for embarrassing me and just wanted to make sure I was all right.'

She bit her lip. 'I'm afraid I was not kind to him. I told him he had blackened Jamie's name by behaving the way he had to his mother. I told him to leave and not come back. I felt bad about saying those things later and went up to his cottage to

183

apologize, but he wasn't there.'

She shook her head. 'He'd come to the boat to make sure I was all right and I sent him packing.' She shrugged, cupping her hands around the warm cup. 'He headed off home. He didn't say anything about going away. I'm really worried.'

Loveday drained her cup and put it back on the saucer and then sat back, thinking. Scobey was a grown man, and if he wanted to take off for a few days why shouldn't he? Then she remembered his obvious concern for Maya. Would he really have deserted her when she needed his support? That didn't sound right. But one thing was sure. Sam would not appreciate having another missing man to check up on.

'How did Jamie meet Scobey?' she asked.

Maya wrinkled her nose, recalling what Jamie had told her. 'It was before Jamie and I met. He'd bought the *April Rose* intending to live on board while renovating her. He got talking to Scobey in the pub and when he described what he was trying to do, Scobey offered to lend a hand.' She looked away. 'He knows all about boats . . . told us he used to have one himself.' She swallowed. 'They had already started work on the *April Rose* when Jamie and I met.'

'Scobey struck me as a very quiet man,' Loveday said.

'I don't know about that. He's certainly a very private man.'

'In what way?'

Maya thought about that for a moment. 'He never talks about his past — before he came to Cornwall, I mean. There's a stillness about him, but you know there is so much more going on in his head.

'He's fit, too. Doesn't even own a car, although Jamie and I both suspected he could well afford to. He rides all over Cornwall on his old mountain bike.' She glanced up. 'That's still there, by the way, at least it was in his shed this morning, and the cottage is still all locked up.'

'What makes you think Scobey isn't short of money?'

'Well, nothing about the way he lives,' Maya said. 'He's practically on bare boards up at his place. There's an old log burner and he chops his own kindling from the woods behind his property. His one and only rug is threadbare, and there never seems to be any food in his fridge.'

She spread her hands. 'Well, you've seen the clothes he wears.'

'He doesn't exactly sound like a man with a secret stash of cash,' Loveday said.

Maya looked up and met her gaze. 'So how come he can afford to have a Stanhope Forbes painting above his bed?'

Loveday recognized the name of a much sought after artist who had painted in Cornwall in the 1920s. She thought most of his work was in galleries. Her eyes widened. 'Has he?'

Maya nodded. 'He's got a Lowry in there, too. I've seen it. Not that I was prying, but the door to his bedroom was open when I visited his loo.' She gave an embarrassed shrug. 'I just happened to notice them.'

'They could have been copies, or even prints,' Loveday suggested.

Maya gave her an indignant look. 'I do know the difference, Loveday. Believe me, those paintings were neither copies nor prints. They were the genuine articles. I studied art at college before I discovered the fascination of archaeology and ancient monuments.'

'And you never mentioned having seen these paintings to him?'

She shook her head. 'Only to Jamie.' A smile crept into the jade coloured eyes. 'He wasn't in the least surprised, but I don't think he knew about Scobey's art collection before I mentioned it. Not that he was bothered. It all added more colour to Jamie's belief that Scobey was a retired spy. He had these old books — political history, sociology, and books about the Middle East, Russia, and China, that kind of stuff. Jamie used to joke about him being a spook from MI6.'

Loveday's eyebrow went up, but Maya shook her head, a twinkle in her eye. 'That was Jamie's little joke. Neither of us believed it for a minute. But Scobey is definitely an intellectual, although he does his best to hide it, which is probably why he never got involved in small talk and gossip.'

Loveday listened in silence. Maya's insight into what made the man tick was fascinating. She could see him sitting in the pub, quietly supping his pint, but listening to everything. It occurred to her that Mr Scobey knew a lot more about the good people of Karrek than even they were aware.

The idea was intriguing. And one she should definitely share with Sam.

She fixed the young woman across the table with an encouraging smile. 'Think, Maya. Are you sure you have no idea where Scobey could have gone?'

Maya gave her a vacant expression. 'None. It's like I said. He never talked about his past, but . . . '

'But what?' Loveday's head shot up.

'I hadn't thought about it until now, but Scobey has a London accent.'

\* \* \*

Everything Maya had told her was still running through Loveday's head as she hurried up the stairs to her office. Her mobile rang. It was Sam. At last! She hadn't heard from him all day.

'Well, hello, stranger. I was beginning to think you'd emigrated,' she said, trying to keep the smile out of her voice.

'Have you missed me?'

'Why do you suppose I've had time to miss you? Have you any idea how much effort goes into putting a magazine together?'

'I'll take that as a no, then.' He actually sounded disappointed. Loveday immediately felt guilty.

'I'm still looking forward to seeing you tonight though. Does that count?'

'It does, and ditto,' Sam said. She could almost hear the smile in his voice.

# 14

'You said what?' Loveday stared at the phone. She had been looking forward to that evening stroll along Marazion beach with Sam as the sun set over the castle.

'Sorry,' he said. 'I was trying to think on my feet. It will only be for an hour or so. I didn't realize you would mind.'

She certainly did mind, but she wasn't going to admit the real reason. 'Have you actually read any of his books?' she said. 'They're gross, Sam.'

'He's a best seller. Somebody must like them.'

Loveday gave a loud sigh. 'The world is full of morons.'

Sam grinned at his phone. 'You're such a snob, Loveday.'

'You really expect me to fawn over this man? I hated his book.'

'Well don't let him know that.'

'You want me to lie?'

190

'Of course not. Just don't say you hated his book.'

She could hear the appealing note in his voice.

'You can do that, can't you?'

'You do realize Maya is convinced Walter Allen killed Jamie,' Loveday said.

'Why would I realize that? What's all this about?'

She was picturing him narrowing his dark eyes, the frown lines on his brow deepening.

'I'm only repeating what Maya said when she came to see me today. Apparently this Walter was forever calling down to see Jamie on the boat without being invited.'

'Hardly evidence of murder,' Sam said.

'But there's more. It seems Walter Allen has been asking questions about Jamie all over the place. Now why would he do that?'

Sam released a heartfelt sigh. 'He could have had his reasons . . . and they could have had nothing to do with Jamie's murder.'

Loveday gave the phone a slow,

suspicious grin. 'You know something, don't you?'

He ignored the comment. 'So are you coming with me to see our writer friend this evening or not?'

It was Loveday's turn to ignore him. 'There's something else you should know, Sam. Tom Scobey has taken off somewhere.' She'd decided that under the circumstances that approach would sound less alarmist than using the 'missing' word.

There was a pause and then Sam said, 'Are you trying to tell me he's disappeared?'

'I've no idea,' Loveday said. 'It was simply something else Maya mentioned. She's worried about him.'

She could tell Sam was trying to decide whether to get his team moving on yet another report of a missing man. But then no one had actually reported him missing.

In fact Sam was kicking himself for not having gone straight back to speak to the man the previous evening, but he and Will had got so involved with interviewing

Sarah and Charles Roscow. The detectives had wanted to know about every aspect of Jamie's life. It had taken time.

There had also been a mountain of paperwork in Sam's inbox, and he'd stayed late trying to organize it.

'How about I pick you up from the office about five and we can go directly to Karrek?' he said. 'I'll ring Allen and confirm we are coming.'

'What about my car?' Loveday asked.

'I can drive you back in the morning.'

'Fine by me,' she said.

They were negotiating the Helston roundabout when Sam asked, 'What else did Maya tell you about Tom Scobey?'

Loveday thought back. 'She said he's a bit of a mystery man. He goes about dressed like a tramp, yet he's apparently well off.'

'Tell me more,' Sam said.

'Maya says he has valuable paintings in his cottage. She's seen a Stanhope Forbes, and another painting by Lowry.'

Sam's mind went back to when he'd first spoken to Tom Scobey on Jamie's boat. The conversation had been brief and the man had given nothing away. Amanda Fox had subsequently interviewed him in his cottage. He would have to revisit her witness report.

'DC Fox didn't mention anything about paintings after she'd spoken to him.'

'According to Maya they are in his bedroom,' Loveday said. 'Apparently she peeked in one time when she was going to the loo in Scobey's cottage.'

'Anything else?'

'That's pretty much it, oh, apart from the fact that he has a London accent, but you would have noticed that for yourself.'

He had, but hadn't attached much importance to it.

He would make a point of calling in on the *April Rose* after seeing Allen.

Walter Allen's house was at the top of an unmade track that wound its way up a wooded hill. Sam brought the Lexus to a halt in a clearing in front of a big white house.

Loveday nodded towards the open garage doors at the side, and the white sporty car she could see there. 'Is that what I think it is?'

Sam glanced at the shiny Aston Martin and let out a low whistle. 'Nice one. Makes my old Lexus look a bit embarrassing.'

They hadn't noticed the house door opening and were startled by the writer's sudden knock on the car window.

'I saw you drive up.' Walter Allen was studying them with calculating dark eyes that took in every detail of his visitors' appearance. He looked exactly as Loveday had imagined him. A slim, immaculate figure in expensive grey calfskin shoes, cream linen jacket, black cords, and a paisley patterned scarf tucked into the open neck of his blue striped shirt. He smoothed a hand over his silver streaked hair and smiled. 'Do come and join us.'

He went to the passenger side of the car and opened the door for Loveday. She glanced back and nodded towards the sports car in the garage.

'If writing crime fiction is this profitable I might have a go at it myself.'

The smile left Walter's face. 'You would

have to go into the publishing business to afford that. It's my wife, Elizabeth's, car.'

Loveday was still thinking about that as the writer ushered them indoors. The place looked like a traditional Cornish house from the outside, but the interior could have been straight from the pages of *Country Life*.

The floors were laid with dark polished wood, and walls had been removed to give an open plan look. Rich red damask curtains hung in elegant swags from ceiling to floor at every window. There were black leather sofas, thick pile cream woollen rugs, and a crystal chandelier twinkling above.

Loveday glanced around her, trying not to give away her dislike of what had been done to the cottage.

'My wife is the interior designer.' Walter gave them another snake-like smile, following Loveday's gaze around the room. 'Clever, isn't she?'

'Your wife has certainly turned this place into something else,' Loveday said, carefully avoiding the sharp look Sam was giving her.

But he needn't have worried, for Walter was still beaming at them. He'd obviously taken her comment as a compliment.

'The Inspector here tells me you are a fan of my Desmond Height novels.'

Loveday blinked. She felt rather than saw Sam's eyes rolling to the ceiling, and wondered if he also had his fingers crossed behind his back. How could she answer this without lying?

She decided to respond with a dazzling smile.

'Writers fascinate me, Mr Allen. Do you actually write your books down here in Cornwall?'

'Mostly I do. I walk a lot.' He bestowed another of his condescending smiles on her. 'I do most of my plotting when I walk down there by the river.' He moved to the window and drew back the expensive drapes, beckoning them to join him.

They did, and Loveday gasped. The wooded slope fell away and the blue water of the Helford Passage sparkled below.

'What an amazing view.' She was trying to equate the inspiration such a vista must surely stimulate with the terrible crime novels this man churned out.

'Come on, I'll show you where I work.' He ushered them out of the room and across the dark hall into a small study that was flooded with light. White painted bookcases lined the walls and an enormous polished oak desk took up most of the floor space. The chair had been placed so that the sitter had his back to the window, which had an even more spectacular view of the estuary.

Walter took in her gaze. 'Beautiful, but distracting,' he said, nodding to the window. 'If I looked out on that I'd get nothing done.'

Loveday glanced around the bookshelves. All of Walter's novels seemed to be there, duplicated in several languages. Her eyes glided over the spines. Desmond Height's name was on almost every one. There was also a wall displaying a selection of framed covers.

She slid Sam a 'how am I doing?' look and caught his slight nod. She decided to try something.

'Are they all fiction?'

Walter narrowed his eyes and for a split

second she thought she detected a flash of discomfort.

'I only write fiction,' he said quickly.

'No, you misunderstand me,' Loveday said. 'I meant did any of your plots actually happen?'

Walter spun round to stare at her. 'I'm not sure I understand.'

She was aware of Sam's warning glance.

'Well, writers do that sometimes, don't they? Isn't it usual for an author to take real life happenings and build a story around them?'

'Ah . . . ' Walter produced what looked remarkably like a relieved smile. 'I see where you're going. But no, I don't do that. My plots come out of my head.' He flashed Sam a grin. 'What you see is what you get. All my own work.'

'Very impressive,' Sam lied. 'But there must be some things that spark an idea?' He was directly facing Walter now. 'Take that fogou where Jamie Roscow's body was found, for instance. Did that not whet your author appetite?'

Walter stared at him. 'Wouldn't that be

in considerably bad taste?'

The door opened and a tall slender woman with long auburn hair came in carrying a tray of drinks. 'My husband refuses to employ help down here in Cornwall,' the newcomer said with a sigh. 'As if the place wasn't uncivilized enough we have to look after ourselves. Is it any wonder I stay up in London?'

Her green eyes swept over Sam's face lingering on his mouth. She completely ignored Loveday.

'This is my wife, Elizabeth,' Walter said. 'She enjoys her little joke.' But he was obviously uncomfortable about her disrespectful entrance.

Loveday cleared her throat. 'Your husband writes so many books Mrs Allen that we were wondering when he finds time to sleep.'

The woman tore her eyes away from Sam. 'It's Callington,' she said sharply. 'Elizabeth Callington. I did not take my husband's name.'

'I'm sorry you don't like Cornwall,' Loveday said. The words all but stuck in her throat. 'I suppose it has some attractions,' Elizabeth said lazily, her eyes sweeping back over Sam. If he felt any embarrassment by the woman's deliberately seductive behaviour he certainly wasn't showing it.

Loveday was struggling with the overwhelming desire to slap the annoying woman. Even Walter was looking uncomfortable. Why was she even here in Cornwall if she hated the place so much?

The message Elizabeth was sending to Sam was unmistakeable.

Loveday drew a breath. She'd had enough of this. 'Mr Allen said you were in publishing,' she said quickly. 'Do you have anyone famous on your books?'

It was a crass statement, but the best she could do under the circumstances. She knew the glib question would irritate Elizabeth. High flyers like her didn't back losers. She was bound to have a stable of only the most successful writers.

Elizabeth turned to look at her, and lifted a delicately pencilled eyebrow. Loveday felt she was being inspected as though she was something unpleasant under foot.

She kept her dislike of the woman in check. 'I mean apart from Mr Allen, of course. I do love a good detective novel. Is that the kind of fiction your publishing house specialises in?' She hated herself for sounding so gushing, but it was the only approach she could think of to get a result.

Elizabeth was still frowning at her, not sure if the questions even merited a response. They were taking her attention away from the delectable man on the other side of the room.

She gave another sigh. 'Which authors did you have in mind?'

Loveday remembered the stack of books on her bedside table. She didn't think this woman would have been remotely familiar with any of the writers she rated. She took another breath and blinked. 'Ian Rankin? Val McDermid?' They were the first author names that came to mind.

'They're not on our list,' Elizabeth said curtly.

'Have you heard of Mike Fanshaw? Neil Conrad? Adam Glen?' It was Walter.

Loveday didn't recognise any of the names, but she flashed him an impressed look anyway and said, 'Wow. Really?'

Ignoring Sam's warning look she turned back to Elizabeth. 'The publishing world must be so exciting, Ms Callington.' She hoped she wasn't overdoing the interest. 'All those high-powered meetings, fast cars, glamorous people. Well just look at you.' Loveday held out her arms as though in admiration of the woman's sleek appearance.

A smile tugged at the edges of the bright red-painted mouth, and Elizabeth inclined her head.

'Maintaining high personal standards goes with the business,' she said.

'I can see that, but you look so young,' Loveday came back, looking her straight in the eye. 'You must have worked so hard to get to the top of the tree, and you are obviously at the top of your business. I expect you have homes all over the world.'

Elizabeth had stopped giving Sam coy looks; she was becoming more engaged with this conversation about herself.

She glanced at Walter. 'We have the London house.'

He inclined his head and smiled back at her.

Elizabeth's gaze slid to the window. 'And I have a place in Malta, a small villa overlooking Valetta Harbour.' A secret smile was playing on her mouth, but the words came out so quietly that Loveday had to strain to catch them. The place obviously meant a lot to her.

'Malta?' Loveday repeated. 'I've never been there.' She was hoping her approach would encourage Elizabeth to say more, but the dismissive cut glass voice was back.

'I've interrupted you. I only came in to leave the drinks.' Elizabeth was shutting down the conversation.

But Sam wasn't ready to let go of it just yet. He gave the woman his most engaging smile. 'Malta?' he repeated.

Elizabeth glanced away, but the flash of annoyance in the green eyes was unmistakeable. She knew she'd already said too much. But why? Why was the subject of Malta apparently dangerous ground for her? She saw Walter frown at his wife.

Sam said, 'Jamie Roscow's parents have a house in Malta, but I'm sure you already know that.'

'I didn't,' Elizabeth's voice was abrupt. 'They never mentioned it.'

Loveday watched the look that passed between the couple and knew Sam had seen it too. He had definitely rattled the woman and if her guarded expression was anything to go by she had expected him to go on with the questions. But he didn't. He changed tack.

'Mr Allen was about to tell us about his research of fogous.' Sam was watching every twinge of the muscles in Walter Allen's face. He could tell he'd hit a nerve. He pressed on. 'That's right isn't it, sir?'

The woman's eyebrow arched a fraction as she looked at her husband. She moved the tray further onto the huge desk. 'I can see I'm not needed here,' she said. 'Do offer your guests some refreshment, Walter. At least do that.'

And with that she left the room.

Walter spun round on his heel and went to the window. He must surely have been embarrassed by his wife's behaviour. Or was he used to it? Loveday suspected it was the latter.

'You will have gathered that my wife does not share my love of Cornwall,' Walter said. 'But the place fascinates me. It's why I bought Hillcrest . . . why I spend so much of my time down here.'

'So you *were* researching fogous?' Sam persisted, not wanting to be dissuaded from his line of questioning.

Walter frowned. 'I thought you and your charming young friend here were interested in my work? But that's not why you're here at all, is it?' He advanced towards Sam, his whole demeanour now threatening. Loveday felt her body stiffen.

'I am investigating a murder, Mr Allen. Have you forgotten?'

Sam could play the intimidating game too.

'Why didn't you tell me you were reporting back to the Roscows?'

Loveday's head jerked up. Sam had kept all this quiet, but why wouldn't he?

206

He didn't take her into his confidence about how his investigation was going. He did expect her to tell him though if she discovered anything that he hadn't known about. She was in two minds about whether to feel annoyed about this.

'You are a lot closer to the Roscows than you led us to believe. You befriended Jamie so you could report every move he made back to his parents.'

'It wasn't like that. I got on with Jamie. I was devastated about what happened.'

'Jamie told you about the fogou, didn't he? He knew you were interested as part of the research for a future book.' Sam paused, locking eyes with Walter. Loveday could feel her heart beating.

'Jamie took you to the fogou, didn't he, Mr Allen?'

Loveday could almost see the man's brain working. He'd lied to the police and now he had to dig himself out of a hole. They waited.

Walter ran his fingers through his silvered hair and gave Sam a defensive look. 'I didn't kill him if that's what you're thinking. I didn't kill Jamie. He was my friend. Why would I hurt him?'

Sam looked down, shifting the weight on his feet. He glanced to the window, studying the view.

'No one has accused you of murdering Jamie, Mr Allen.' He swung round, fixing Walter with an unblinking stare. 'Now why would you think that?'

Loveday watched with fascination as the man attempted to bluster his way out of the situation. For an innocent man, he sure was looking guilty.

Sam's almost imperceptible gesture beckoned her towards the door. But as they reached it he spun back round. 'Just one more thing, Mr Allen. Do you know Tom Scobey?'

Walter frowned. 'Scobey?'

'Yes, you know . . . greying hair in a ponytail, faded jeans, shabby waistcoat. He helped Jamie on his boat.'

'Oh yes, him. I know who you mean. What about him?'

Sam shrugged. 'Only that he's disappeared.' He looked directly at Walter and saw the muscles in his neck twitch.

'I thought you might have known that.'

# 15

'Say thank you then,' Loveday said as they drove away from Walter's cottage. But Sam was frowning, deep in thought. She knew better than to distract him at times like these, but still, she felt a little glow of satisfaction. The writer hadn't known about Scobey's disappearance, and judging by the reaction he'd tried so desperately to cover, it was evidently significant.

She sat in silence as they reached the bottom of the hill, expecting Sam to turn left, away from the village, but he swung the big car down towards the creek.

A thin curl of smoke rose from the narrowboat's chimney. Sam pulled the Lexus off the path and killed the engine. 'Any chance of you waiting here in the car while I have a word with Maya?'

Loveday gave him a wordless stare.

'You shouldn't really be with me when I interview a witness, Loveday. You know that.'

'You wouldn't have known anything about Scobey's disappearance if it hadn't been for me.'

'We would have done . . . eventually,' he countered.

'But I've given you a head start. Admit it, Sam. I could tell from Walter's reaction that something important is going on here.' The earnest look she gave him wrinkled her brow.

Sam gave a resigned sigh. 'OK, you can come. But don't say anything.'

Loveday held up her hands in defence. And Sam pointed a finger at her. 'I mean it, Loveday . . . not a word.'

If Maya was surprised to see them she gave no clue. She looked too defeated for that. Alarm bells were ringing in Loveday's head. She touched the girl's arm. 'Something's happened, hasn't it?'

Sam shot her a frown. Hardly a second across the threshold and already she was interfering. She knew how annoyed he would be, but she felt responsible for this young woman. It was her she'd confided in after all, not Sam.

'Come and sit down,' she said, trying to

avoid Sam's eyes as she led Maya back down the steps and into the boat's saloon. But he was immediately behind them, and nodding to her. Was he actually giving her permission to carry on? She didn't wait to find out. 'Tell us what's happened, Maya,' she said gently.

Maya pointed. 'It's over there.'

Loveday and Sam followed her direction to a letter on the low table.

'It was left for me at the pub.' She got up and went to pick up the note, offering it to Sam, but he indicated she should put it back on the table. He didn't want to contaminate possible evidence by getting his own fingerprints all over the paper. Maya watched his eyes scan the sheet as Loveday looked over his shoulder. The writing was a long, loopy scrawl.

'*Dear Maya,*

*Had to get away to sort my head out about Jamie. Don't worry about me. I am fine.*'

'I don't understand,' Sam said. 'He's just telling you he's going away, and not to worry.'

Maya stared at him. 'So how come he left the note *after* he'd already gone?'

Sam and Loveday exchanged a confused look.

'What do you mean?' Sam asked.

'I went up to Scobey's place last night. I wanted to apologize for how I'd spoken to him earlier, and to show him Jamie's painting, the one Loveday and Keri brought. He wasn't there. The cottage was all locked up.'

Loveday tried to ignore the frown Sam was firing in her direction. She hadn't told him about the painting. She said, 'Mr Scobey could have gone shopping.'

'Not without his bike. I told you, it was still propped up in the shed at the side of the cottage.'

She swallowed. 'He didn't come down to the boat this morning either, which was odd because he looked in on me every morning. When he still hadn't showed up by lunchtime I went back to the cottage. He hadn't been back. That's when I realized he'd gone.' She looked at Loveday. 'And that's when I came in to tell you.'

'But the note, he left you a note,' Loveday said.

Maya nodded. 'Seth Vingoe, the pub landlord brought the note to me himself. He said it was pushed through his door this morning. So how come Scobey was pushing notes through the door of the Badger Inn this morning when I know he hasn't been in the village since last night?'

'How can you be so certain he didn't come back and go away again?' Loveday asked.

'Because I pushed a note of my own into the cottage letter box when I went up there last evening and a tiny corner got trapped by the spring. The letter was still there this morning. I went up especially to check after Seth brought the note.'

She turned glistening eyes on Sam. 'I'm really worried, Inspector. I don't know what it means.'

Sam was deep in thought. The landlord could have lied about when he'd received the note. But why would he? If Maya was right, and Scobey really hadn't left the note, it didn't make any sense. He glanced back at the scribbled lines. Could it be that someone didn't want them digging into Tom Scobey's life — and did that someone know where the missing man was now?

'There's more,' Maya said, grabbing the letter and waving it at them. 'Scobey never wrote this. It's simply not the kind of thing he would say.'

She looked from one to the other. 'Well, don't you see? If Scobey didn't send it then who did? And Why?'

Exactly what Loveday had been thinking, and she could tell Sam was curious about it too. If the thing was thought out logically, and Scobey really hadn't sent the note, then perhaps whoever did was trying to stop Maya looking for him.

The same thought had obviously occurred to Sam for he said, 'Are you sure you know absolutely nothing about Scobey's past?' His mind was again tracking through the conversation he'd had with the man. Had he missed any clues there?

Sam glanced back to the letter. 'Do you have a plastic bag, Maya?'

The young woman's eyes widened. 'Oh

my God! You think something's happened to him.' She clamped her hand to her mouth.

Sam looked at Loveday and she saw the concern in his eyes. 'It's a routine precaution. I'll get our forensic people to check it for fingerprints. You mustn't read any more into it.'

But Loveday knew it was more than that.

'Did Scobey have any special friends that you know of?' Sam asked.

'Not really. He didn't like company. He said people only let him down.'

'And yet he struck up a relationship with you and Jamie?'

Maya's brow wrinkled. 'Yes, but I hadn't thought about it before. Jamie and I really liked Scobey. He was always around, but if I'm honest . . . ' Her words trailed off. She frowned. 'I suppose you could say his relationship was more with the boat than with us.'

Loveday stared at her in surprise. That wasn't the impression she'd got the day she and Sam met him. He'd looked as worried as Maya when Sam told them that a body had been found, and that it could be Jamie.

Maya had turned to take a roll of plastic bags from a drawer in the table. She tore one off and handed it to Sam.

'Is the letter evidence?'

He smiled at her. 'Just belt and braces at this stage. It's probably nothing, but we'll check it out anyway.'

They'd been about to leave when Sam turned back to Maya. 'I understand Mr Scobey has some valuable works of art in his cottage?'

Maya shot Loveday a glance and got an encouraging nod in return.

'That's right — a Stanhope Forbes and an L.S. Lowry. He has good taste.'

'Could Jamie have bought them for him? I understand his family is wealthy.'

Maya looked surprised. 'Of course not. Jamie took nothing from his parents, and he certainly couldn't afford to buy expensive works of art for Scobey. Why would he?'

Sam shrugged. 'Only a thought.'

But it added extra confusion.

He looked at Maya. 'I don't suppose

you have a key for Scobey's cottage?'

She shook her head. 'No, but if you're going up there I'm coming with you.'

Sam had been about to tell Loveday to stay with Maya on the boat while he went off to check out the cottage, but it struck him that it might be helpful to have the young woman with him. If there was anything untoward she was more likely to spot it than him.

He nodded. 'Let's go.'

Maya led the way through the woods to the isolated property. Loveday was sure that if she hadn't known it was there she would never have found it. The uphill climb on the rough path had made them all a bit breathless. Suddenly it was there in front of them. Not the prettiest cottage she'd ever seen.

'It used to be the woodcutter's place,' Maya said. 'Jamie told me it had been lying empty for years before Scobey moved in.'

The man had apparently been renovating it.

Sam's eyes travelled over the small stone building. It had been given a coat of white paint, but it hadn't disguised the fact that the place needed more serious attention. There were windows on either side of the peeling green painted door. He stepped back and looked up. He could see moss growing on the roof tiles and around the two attic windows. The cottage looked secure enough, but it had a sad, neglected appearance.

'Stay here,' he instructed. 'I'll have a scout round the back.'

'Not without us,' Loveday said.

Sam raised an eyebrow then decided any argument he put up would be pointless.

He walked round the building, and then stopped dead. A window had been broken. The pane of glass was small, but it would have allowed someone to put a hand in and slide the snib. Tom Scobey's cottage had been broken into.

'Is this what I'm thinking it is?' Loveday's eyes were also on the broken glass.

'I'm going to try to get in,' Sam said, carefully sliding his own hand through the shattered glass and releasing the catch, allowing the window to swing free.

He had been about to try to squeeze in when Maya stepped forward.

'You'll never fit in there,' she said. 'Let me try.'

Sam didn't like the idea. It wouldn't look good if the girl injured herself doing something he had condoned. On the other hand she was right. His shoulders were far too broad to fit through that small space.

He took a clean hankie from his pocket and gave it to Maya.

'Try to touch as little as possible and use this to open the back door.' The last thing he wanted was her fingerprints on the handle confusing the forensic team he would be calling in. She took the hankie and he gave her a leg up, standing back as she disappeared into the cottage. Almost immediately the back door creaked open and Maya stood there with an excited grin. 'I'm in,' she said.

Sam was about to step over the threshold when he stopped. 'This is a crime scene so I have to ask you both to wait outside.' He looked from one to the other. 'You do understand that?'

Loveday frowned, but she knew Sam had no option. Maya nodded.

'Let me have a look around first. If it's safe inside I'll let you know.' For all he knew there could be a body in here, and he certainly didn't want either of the women to be the ones to discover it.

He was in a dark hallway with a kitchen to his left. On his immediate right a set of stairs led up presumably to bedrooms. He glanced into the kitchen but could see no sign of damage. Another room led off it. He went through, but saw nothing out of place. A cable on the floor caught his eye. It was still plugged into a socket on the wall, but the computer that had once been attached to it was missing.

Careful not to disturb anything he headed upstairs. He only wanted a cursory look around, mainly to see if that Stanhope Forbes painting, and the Lowry were still there. They weren't. Whoever it was that had broken into Tom Scobey's cottage knew exactly what they were after.

Loveday stared impatiently at him as he came out. 'Well, what did you find?'

'The paintings Maya talked about are missing.' He turned to the smaller woman. 'Did Scobey have a computer?'

Maya nodded. 'In that little room off the kitchen. He used it as a kind of office.'

Sam gave a grim smile. 'That's gone too.'

# 16

Sam's team was waiting for him as he came into the briefing room next morning. It was five days since the discovery of Jamie's body, and they were no closer to making an arrest than they had been on day one. If it went on like this they would all be working over the coming weekend, which was not great for the family lives of his team.

His first marriage to Victoria had ended primarily because he was never there, but workloads even back then had been ridiculously heavy. And although his former first wife and his children lived in Plymouth, he didn't see them nearly as often as he would have liked. His son, Jack, was fourteen now, and daughter, Maddie, almost eleven. He sighed. Long hours went with the job. At least Loveday understood that.

He looked round the faces of his officers and thanked them for coming in so early, and then quickly got down to business.

'Three things,' he said. 'First we need to check that the Roscows really were out of the country when their son was killed.

'And second, we need to speak to Walter Allen again.'

'Would you like me to do that, boss?' DC Amanda Fox offered.

Sam hadn't needed to imagine what that interview would have been like. It wasn't a good idea.

He smiled and shook his head. 'I want you to check up on the Roscows. Go out and have a word with them. Will and I will call in on Allen.' He ignored the look of disappointment on the young detective's face.

Turning to the third member of his team, DC Malcolm Carter, he said, 'Have we turned up anything on Tom Scobey's whereabouts yet?'

'Nothing so far, boss. There's no trace of any bank account, he's not registered with any local GP, and he doesn't seem to have a National Insurance number, at least not under the name Scobey.'

Sam's brow furrowed. He was thinking about that break-in and the paintings that had gone missing. It was possible that Tom Scobey had set the whole thing up himself. It could be an elaborate insurance scam. Was Scobey capable of that? He didn't know, but somehow he didn't think so.

The briefing lasted another twenty minutes and broke up when all the officers on the Jamie Roscow murder enquiry were clear what their duties were for the day.

Sam went back to his office and stood for a moment gazing out at the dreary view of a car park before opening the bulky files in front of him. It was all so familiar — the post mortem report, the forensics, the photos of the crime scene, and the victim.

He stared at Jamie Roscow's boyish, handsome face. It was a nice face, open and friendly. The eyes were friendly too, pale grey and candid. There was something about those eyes. Sam tilted his head and looked at the photo from a different angle. Jamie Roscow had looked nothing like his parents, so why were those eyes so familiar?

He closed his own eyes and pinched the bridge of his nose, hoping the headache that was just starting would pass.

He tried to work out who those eyes reminded him of, but nothing came.

He flicked through the other photographs in the file, pausing when he reached Walter Allen's picture.

It looked like one of the author's posed professional shots. Allen's body was angled away from the camera, the sharp-featured face was unsmiling and the eyes staring out to some object in the distance. The background was the bookcase Sam remembered from his and Loveday's visit to the man's house in Karrek.

★   ★   ★

Loveday was in her friend, Laura Bennington's, tiny office in the museum in Truro, where they were drinking peppermint tea from delicate china cups.

'What do you know about fogous, Laura?'

'Not a lot,' Laura said, 'apart from being aware that fogou is a Cornish word for cave. I'm not an archaeologist.'

'But you're the curator of this museum.' Loveday held her arms aloft and indicated the vaulted ceilings. 'You must know something. I'm depending on you.'

Laura narrowed her eyes. 'OK, Loveday. What's this all about? You don't really want to know about fogous, do you?'

She leaned forward, focusing on her friend's unconvincing stare.

'Would you believe I'm writing an article on Cornish antiquities?'

Laura raised an eyebrow. 'And Merrick agreed to this?'

Loveday smiled. 'He's humouring me.'

'Why's he doing that?'

'Why are you being so suspicious?'

'Because I know you, Loveday, and you're up to something.'

Loveday looked away, stifling an embarrassed grin. She put up her hands in mock surrender. 'Guilty as charged.'

Laura waited for her to go on.

'The thing is I've inherited a fogou.' She ignored her friend's look of surprise and went on, 'It's on a site where my family once had a cottage. The building is now a pile of rubble, but . . . ' She paused, not sure she should finish what she'd started.

'Well, don't stop there,' Laura said.

Loveday sighed and pulled a face. 'The thing is . . . it's the same fogou where the body of that young man was found.'

Laura put down her cup and stared at her. 'So is this article thing really a cover for you doing your own investigation?'

'Not exactly.'

'What then?'

'I suppose I feel involved. It was Sam and I who found him . . . the dead man, I mean. And he only happened to be a friend of Keri and Ben.'

'Never!' Laura's eyes widened. 'So what does Sam think about all this?'

'Nothing. Why would he think anything of it? I'm not doing anything that compromises his case. I already know most of the people involved anyway.'

Laura sighed. 'Seriously Loveday. Is

this a good idea? What could you possibly gain from getting involved in a murder? Leave it to Sam.'

'I'm not getting involved. I told you. I need to speak to these people anyway for the article, which is why I'm here . . . remember? I need to pick your brain about antiquities.'

Laura gave an exasperated sigh. 'OK, if you're determined to go on with this then I can put you in touch with someone.' She paused. 'In fact . . . ' She put a finger in the air. 'I probably do have something for you. But I need your word to keep this confidential, for the moment anyway.'

Loveday nodded. 'Of course.'

'There's a farmer out on the Lizard who has unearthed an ancient barrow.' She paused again. 'With his digger, would you believe?'

'What's a barrow?'

Laura gave another sigh. 'For a journalist you don't know very much, do you?'

'I do, actually. I just don't know what a barrow is. I'm assuming it's not the thing with handles that you wheel round the garden?'

'It's an ancient burial site where the bodies of important members of the community were placed in stone vaults and covered with mounds of earth. This particular one could date back to the early Bronze Age circa 1900 BC.'

'And one has been discovered on the Lizard?'

'That's right.' Laura nodded. 'We keep important locations like this a secret to protect them from being plundered. You've heard of nighthawks?'

Loveday had. She knew they were unprincipled people with metal detectors who had no qualms about raiding ancient sites to dig up artefacts and sell them on to private collectors. They basically dealt in destroying priceless archaeological relics.

'I can see why you need to be discreet. I don't like these people any more than you.'

'I'm sure you don't, Loveday, which is why I'm trusting you.'

Loveday nodded, focusing her attention on Laura's face.

'The Cornwall Archaeological Trust has a base here at the museum. I'll have a word with Zara Barfett — she's the secretary, but she's also an archaeologist in her own right — and I'll ask her to contact you.'

'That would be brilliant, Laura. Thank you.'

*   *   *

Zara Barfett was a small, pert-featured young woman with a bouncy blonde bob and a personality to match. She was wearing a sunshine yellow tee shirt and denim shorts as she came forward to greet Loveday in the museum cafe that afternoon. Her smile revealed dazzling white teeth, making Loveday wonder how she kept them that way.

'Coffee?' she asked.

'Only if I can pay for them.' Loveday smiled. Why hadn't she met this girl before? She was already planning the future article she would write about her and her work.

'I gather Laura has told you about our

barrow?' she said as their coffees arrived.

Loveday nodded. 'And she's also explained the need to keep the location of the site secret. No one will learn it from me.'

Zara was studying her face. 'That's what Laura said, and now that I've met you it's good enough for me.' She heaped three spoons of Demerara sugar into her cup and said, 'Now what do you want to know?'

'As much as you can tell me,' Loveday said. 'I understand the barrow was unearthed by a local farmer?'

'On the Lizard, that's right,' Zara explained. 'His name's George Pawley. He was turning over one of his fields at — ' She hesitated, as though still unsure about revealing too much. But she must have decided that Loveday really could be trusted because she continued, 'It's Carrick Farm. As I was saying, he was working on one of his fields, turning the soil over with a digger when it scooped up what he initially thought were rocks. I suppose they were really, but they turned out to be a lot more interesting than he could ever imagine.'

Loveday waited as Zara sipped some more of her coffee and put the cup back on the saucer.

'For years George had only used that field for grazing, but this time he'd decided to put a crop in there. He hired a digger to take up the rough grass but so many old stones were coming up in the bucket that he was wondering if he'd done the right thing.' She smiled. 'He got down from the digger to have a closer look and it was then that he realized this was something more than simply a stony field. Once the top covering of grass and earth had been removed he could see a straight ridge to the stones. He said they looked as if they had been built into the site.'

'That was very observant of him,' Loveday said.

Zara nodded. 'Apparently George is quite interested in archaeology. He'd always known there were ancient monuments on the Lizard peninsula, but he'd never heard anything about having one on his own farm.

'He rang the museum and spoke to Laura, and she passed the information on to me.' She beamed Loveday another brilliant smile. 'I went out to have a look, and guess what? It was a fabulous ancient barrow. I could hardly contain my excitement.'

'So what happens now? Will you excavate it?'

Zara clasped a hand to her chest and her lovely blue eyes shone. 'I can't wait.'

'So nothing has happened yet?'

'Sadly no. There's quite a bit of red tape to go through before we can move in and do our work, but we're counting the days.'

'And you're quite happy for me to go out there and speak to Mr Pawley?'

'Of course. Like I said. You're a friend of Laura's and I trust you. The only stipulation is that you don't disturb the site.'

Loveday placed a hand on her heart and laughed. 'I promise.'

Carrick Farm on the Lizard was a good hour's drive away on a day like this. Journeys around Cornwall always took longer when the roads were busy with tourists.

She toyed with looking for a telephone number for the farmer, but convinced herself that George Pawley would have a mobile and there was no way she could access that without prior knowledge. Anyway, Zara would have informed him of this visit so he would be expecting her.

She had texted Keri from the museum, informing her that something unexpected had turned up and she was on her way to an interview. It was all a bit cloak and dagger, but she didn't want to say anything about the barrow until she'd been out there.

As she crept along behind the long stream of vehicles heading towards Helston she was already beginning to feel excited. She followed the traffic to the roundabout and turned right, passing RNAS Culdrose naval base. After that much of the slow moving traffic began streaming off to beaches at Coverack and Mullion Cove, making the latter part of her journey along the peninsula easier.

The sat nav took her off the main road

to the left and along a narrow lane. Half a mile further on she was driving into the muddy yard of Carrick Farm.

George Pawley was coming towards her, an arm out to warn her off.

'I'm not doing any interviews,' he called gruffly.

Loveday stopped the car and stepped out onto the mud. She gazed in despair at the mess on her lovely red shoes and sighed. 'Mr Pawley?' The farmer frowned at her but didn't deny who he was. 'Didn't Zara Barfett tell you I was coming?

'I'm not a newspaper journalist. I'm from *Cornish Folk* — the magazine — and I'm working on a feature about ancient Cornish relics.'

The farmer's previously hostile expression relaxed a little, but it didn't run to a smile.

He said, 'I'd like to help you out, but I've been told not speak to the press.'

'So Zara hasn't phoned you?'

'I've been out in the fields all afternoon.'

'Well, I'm sure when you check your

phone you'll find that Zara has left a message telling you it's OK to speak to me.'

'Really?' He was still regarding her with suspicion. He glanced back at the farmhouse, and then back to her. 'Wait here,' he instructed, striding off across the yard and disappearing into the low stone building. It was five minutes before he reappeared, and he looked as though he had washed.

'Yeah . . . there was a message from Zara on my answerphone,' he said reluctantly. 'I suppose it's all right to speak to you.'

Loveday sighed. At last!

They walked out across the field and the man listened intently as she told him about the land she had inherited, and the ancient fogou that was on the site.

'So maybe you can understand why this is especially important to me?' she said.

He nodded. 'It's fine. I get it. But I'm still not happy about taking you out here.'

'Would it help if I promise to be very careful where I step?' she said appealingly.

'Sorry, Miss, I don't really think . . . '

But he was definitely wavering.

She shot out her hand, hoping her smile would finally persuade him that she could be trusted. 'I don't think I introduced myself,' she said. 'I'm Loveday.'

George Pawley took it, and scratched his tousled head with his other hand.

'I promise not to get under your feet,' Loveday continued. 'Just a quick look at the site and then I'll be on my way.'

The farmer stared out over his fields with wary grey eyes, and then he nodded. 'Five minutes then . . . no more.'

'That's all I need.' Loveday grinned. 'Lead the way.'

The scatter of stones reminded her of the land she'd inherited. She drew her eyebrows together. 'What made you suspect you'd found something important?'

'I'll show you,' he said, striding out ahead. She hurried after him. He pointed. 'There.'

She followed his direction and saw what he meant. There was a definite pattern to the way the stones had been placed, but it was hardly spectacular.

'And the archaeologists believe this is a Bronze Age barrow?'

The farmer nodded. 'They got quite excited.' He scratched his head again. 'Don't see what all the fuss is about though, but I suppose the site is very old.'

Loveday was trying to work out if it would be worth taking a picture or not. It would be different if there was an actual archaeological dig taking place, but to her uninformed mind, this was just a heap of old stones and rubble.

She stepped back and suddenly the ground wobbled beneath her foot. A huge hole was opening up around her. George Pawley lunged forward and made a grab for Loveday, managing to pull her back before she tumbled into the alarmingly widening pit.

She clutched at her chest, panting.

'Are you all right?' George said, his face crumpled with concern.

It had all happened so quickly that she'd bypassed the surprised stage. But now she could feel her pulse throbbing. Her hand went to her throat. 'What happened?' She now realized the ground hadn't caved in more than a couple of feet, but it had felt like an earthquake.

She stared into the hole and at her mobile phone lying at the bottom amongst the newly exposed soil.

'I'll get it,' the farmer said. But Loveday stopped him from stepping down into the hole.

'No, wait!' she said. 'It might not be stable down there. I'm a bit lighter than you. Let me get the phone.'

She put out a hand for him to steady her as she carefully inched her way down. The freshly revealed earth smelled damp and musty. She bent her knees and reached out gingerly for the phone until her fingers closed around it.

As she began to straighten up, something caught her eye . . . an object sticking out of the wall. She shivered. Oh my God! What was that? She reached out for George Pawley's hand again, but as she attempted to climb out of the hole, the entire side of it collapsed.

Loveday could hear her own screams as the darkness came down.

She didn't think she had passed out, for she could hear the farmer's panicky voice gasping for breath.

'Miss Loveday? Are you all right?'

He had jumped into the hole and was frantically working to dig her out.

Gradually light appeared from the darkness. She could feel the earth being more gently brushed from her face. She scrunched up her eyes, blinking out the grit. Her hands were free and she made a grab for the phone she could see sticking out of the loose earth. As her fingers closed on it, she felt something small and sharp also in her grip.

Strong hands reached down to her, grabbing her under the arms and hoisting her out of the debris.

She'd tried to close her eyes, shutting out the horror of what she had seen down there, but the image wouldn't go away.

She slumped on the ground, gasping.

'Hand the phone over,' George said. 'I'll call an ambulance.'

Loveday waved an arm at him. 'No. I'm fine.' She hesitated. 'It's the police we need!'

The farmer stared at her. 'What are you talking about?'

Loveday released her grip on her phone and opened her hand. A small shiny object lay in her palm beside the phone.

'It's a diamond ring,' she said, staring down at it. 'And that's not a setting from ancient times.'

George blinked, his brow creasing. 'I don't understand. How did it get down there?'

Loveday's eyes slid back to the pit. 'I think it was on the body that's buried down there.'

# 17

It was half an hour before the first vehicle arrived. Loveday saw it stop on the narrow road across the field and watched the two officers get out and stride towards them. One was tall and thin. The other older man was shorter and heavier. In different circumstances she thought they would have looked comical walking side by side like that.

George Pawley heaved a loud sigh. 'They're going to turn this into a circus, aren't they?'

'I'm sure they will be respectful,' Loveday said, knowing they probably wouldn't. If this turned out to be a murder scene — and it was certainly looking that way — the field would soon be overrun with heavy boots and people in white forensic suits. The area would be taped off, and a tent would be erected over the immediate site. She expected there would be floodlights too. The

Scenes of Crime team would need the light to collect and photograph evidence.

Zara's smiling face came into her mind. She wouldn't be smiling either once she found out about this.

'Can you both step back, please?' The shorter rotund officer was taking charge.

'This is my land,' George Pawley snapped indignantly. 'So you can stop ordering me about. I'm staying right here.'

The officer gave him a tight-lipped frown. He could have reeled off the stuff about obstructing the police, but Pawley and the young woman with him were already standing well back from the subsidence.

He moved forward and peered into the hole. 'So where's this skeleton then?' he asked.

Loveday pointed. 'It's just there . . . on the left side near the bottom.'

Both officers moved closer to the edge and gazed down.

The tall one spotted it immediately and his lip curled in distaste. 'We'll have to call this in, Steve.'

He turned, addressing Loveday and the farmer. 'What is this place?'

'It's an ancient burial site,' Loveday chipped in before Pawley could utter a word.

'Burial site? Is that what this is?'

She could see how the man's mind was working. Skeletons were to be expected in places like this. Why had they rung the police?

She stepped forward and opened her hand, displaying the sparkly ring.

'This was with the skeleton. I'm no expert on Bronze Age jewellery, but I'm guessing this isn't it.' She squinted up at the officer. 'It's modern.'

The PC tugged a less than pristine white hankie from his trouser pocket and nodded for Loveday to drop the ring into it. She did.

The other officer was already reaching for his handset.

Loveday heard his professional even tone as he gave details of what was lying at the bottom of the hole. She saw him nod at the phone as the call ended.

He turned to look at her, taking in her

mud-stained clothes and the cuts and grazes he could see on her hands and her ashen-white face. 'I think you need to sit down, young lady. I'll take you back to your car. I'm guessing it's the white Clio back in the farmyard?'

Loveday nodded. She wasn't happy about being led off the site, but the officer was right. Her legs were shaky and she was feeling distinctly queasy.

'CID will want to speak to you when they get here. Will you be all right on your own for a bit?'

She'd be better if the man would stop treating her like a child. 'I'll be absolutely fine,' she said more sharply than she'd intended. 'I do know the procedure.'

The constable gave her a funny look, but he was too anxious to get back to his duties to ask what she'd meant.

As she watched him hurry away back across the field, Loveday got out her phone and dictated everything that had happened, including her feeling of horror when she realized she was staring at the eye sockets of a skeleton.

She thought of ringing Sam but

decided against it. He would probably be on the way anyway.

His silver Lexus was the first vehicle she saw bumping up the rough track and ran out to meet him.

His surprise turned to alarm when he saw her injuries, and how dishevelled she looked.

She gave him a sheepish grin. 'Now don't get annoyed, Sam. It wasn't my fault that that thing was down there. I was only doing my job.'

He shook his head and grinned down at her, putting an arm round her shoulders and walking her back to her car, where he sat her down and stood by the open door. 'Care to tell me what happened?'

By the time she had finished relating her story other police vehicles were pulling into the yard.

Sam glanced across at them. 'I'll have to go,' he said. 'Someone will come back to take your statement.' He tilted her chin up until she met his gaze. 'Are you sure you're OK?'

Loveday laughed. 'I'm fine, so you can

stop fussing.' She wasn't going to tell him she rather liked to be fussed over.

In the end it wasn't a member of his team who came back to take her statement. It was Sam himself.

'Do you feel like going through it again?' he said gently.

She swallowed, trying to banish the image of that skeleton from her mind, but it always came flashing back. She hadn't seen it until the side of the hole caved in, and suddenly there it was, embedded in the soil. And now she couldn't get that picture out of her head.

'I don't know what else I can tell you, Sam. The ground just gave way and I would have fallen in if Mr Pawley hadn't grabbed me.' She took a breath.

'And then I saw my phone down in the bottom of the hole and went in to retrieve it.' She swallowed. 'That was when the side of the hole caved in and I saw it . . . ' Her bottom lip trembled.

Sam put his arms around her. 'It's OK, Loveday. I shouldn't have asked you to be so explicit. It was insensitive.'

'No, I know you have to ask. I don't

know what else to say. Will you get any information from the ring?'

'Maybe,' Sam said. His brow creased. 'There was an inscription.'

Loveday looked up. 'What did it say?'

'*For precious secrets.*'

'Well, I suppose that's better than from John to Mary with love, but it's all a bit cryptic. What do you think?'

Sam shrugged. 'It could be a quote from a book I suppose.'

'Or a gift for keeping quiet about an affair?' Loveday said. 'I suppose there's no doubt that the ring belongs to the body?'

'No guarantees,' Sam said. 'But it's unlikely whoever buried the body chucked the ring in after them.'

'So the person was wearing the ring?'

'Seems likeliest.'

'Which would mean the skeleton is definitely a woman?'

Sam nodded.

'When will you know how long it's been down there?'

'Dr Bartholomew has promised to give us a ballpark date this afternoon. If it's recent then we'll check our missing persons file.'

'She might not be Cornish though. She could be from anywhere and just been dumped here.'

'Let's hope not.'

Loveday thought for a moment and then said, 'You don't suppose . . . ?' She shook her head. 'No, that wouldn't make sense.'

'What?'

'Well, I was thinking. What if our lady wasn't dumped randomly?'

'What do you mean?'

'Could whoever buried her have chosen the site because he or she knew its significance?'

Sam stared at her, frowning. 'I think you're letting your journalistic imagination run away with you. If it had been widely known that this was a Bronze Age site then the archaeological society would surely have been aware of it before now.'

'I'm not suggesting that, Sam.' She took a breath. 'What if our murderer — and it has to be a murder, doesn't it?'

'Not necessarily,' Sam interrupted.

'Our lady could have died naturally, or accidentally.'

Loveday shook her head. 'Then why bury her at all? And I keep coming back to why there? The choice of that particular place must be significant. And if so, then our perpetrator must have known about its significance.'

For a few minutes neither of them spoke. Loveday chewed her bottom lip, thinking this over.

'So maybe we're looking for someone who knows about archaeology . . . I mean really knows.'

Sam thought about this and then shook his head. 'That wouldn't make sense unless he, or she, wanted to be found out. It would be like chucking clues at us.'

'Maybe not. He, or she, probably didn't suspect the site would be discovered. Remember, it was a complete fluke that George Pawley uncovered the barrow. No one could have predicted that would happen.'

Sam wasn't sure he'd go along with that. 'I'm still not convinced,' he said.

'Why chose a particular site like that to bury a body?'

'Arrogance? One-upmanship? Showing off? I don't know. You're the detective, Sam.'

'Exactly, and you're the journalist. I deal in facts, not fancy.'

'You think my theory is fanciful?'

'Don't you?'

Loveday sighed. He was right. Her idea was far-fetched. If the local archaeological society hadn't known about this barrow — and they obviously hadn't, at least not before the farmer had alerted them — how could anyone else have known?

'I wonder if our farmer has had any trespassers on his land lately,' Loveday wondered.

'What does that have to do with this?'

'Probably nothing. I was thinking out loud.'

'The body didn't go into its grave any time recently,' Sam said.

'Obviously not.' Loveday frowned at him. 'But maybe whoever did put it there was checking up that it hadn't been disturbed. She looked up at him. 'It's still worth a try isn't it? I mean, you don't exactly have too many other clues.'

'I don't exactly regard that as a clue.' He sighed. 'We'll obviously be talking to Mr Pawley.'

'Good,' she said. 'And when you do you might ask him if he has any other important bits of archaeology on his land.'

# 18

William Bentley lifted the silver framed photograph from the top of the antique secretaire and hurled it across the room. It smashed into the corner, sending a burst of splinters over the green wool carpet. He stared after it; the glass on the beautiful face had fragmented into a thousand pieces, distorting the lovely blue eyes, and the smile of an angel.

He didn't notice the tears rolling down his cheeks, and if he had he wouldn't have cared. They had been soul mates until she betrayed him. She shouldn't have done that.

And now she had spoiled everything else, leaving him with nothing. She had destroyed his life.

He stared at the shattered image and his upper lip curled into a sneer.

'You have to pay for this. You know that, don't you?'

The words were forced out. Icy

. . . jagged . . . brittle.

'It's all your fault. You made this happen. You killed us!' He continued muttering to himself as he paced the room, planning how he could destroy her.

It hadn't always been this painful. It had been good in the early days. He'd enjoyed the excitement of the clandestine meetings, the ecstatic pleasures they had shared together. Would that passion between them have been diminished if their affair had become public? He would never know now, for it never had. She had ended it long before then. He'd known in his heart that it wouldn't last forever. Good things never did.

William had never blamed her for going back to her husband, not that she had ever really left him. He'd realized that, after those early weeks of pain when there had seemed no point in going on living without her. But he *had* lived — and he had prospered.

Pouring all his energy into his career in merchant banking had reaped its financial rewards. It paid for his Kensington flat and all the beautiful antiques he'd filled it with. He enjoyed going to the upmarket auctions and if, at the back of his mind, he had any thought of meeting her there, he quickly buried it.

In the early days after the split he'd told himself he didn't care about her any more, but he still scanned the society pages of the glossy magazines looking for her face and took some comfort from the fact that it wasn't there.

Had she withdrawn from the high life, still nursing a longing for them to be together again? She had ended their relationship because she could no longer cope with the guilt of cheating on her husband. At least that's what she'd told him. Had he believed her? He wasn't sure. The only certain thing was that she'd chosen her husband, and deserted him.

And then he'd read that they had adopted a child. He tried to force the images of their happy family from his mind. He was no part of it, and the pain of that tore him apart.

Getting out of the city would have been too much like running away, so he'd stayed. His love of antiques had extended into fine art, and over the years he'd built up a collection to be envied. William was particularly proud of the Cornish scenes by an artist whose work he much admired, Walter Langley.

He couldn't remember when he'd finally made the decision to move out of London and leave his old life behind. It had surprised even him, for until then he had been single-minded about his career, and amassing the fortune he now had.

The trappings of wealth attracted him. He loved the yacht that he kept in a mooring at St Katherine Docks, but sailing no longer held the same pleasure for him. And yet he hadn't sold it, and he had kept the apartment. Perhaps now he would let them go. These things belonged to the past and he didn't care for any of that any more. Money meant nothing to him now. If he was honest, it probably never had. It wasn't the money; it was the making of it that had always attracted him. He'd been hooked on the drug of success. It was the achievement he'd been addicted to.

But as the years passed, that had also ebbed away and he'd been left with the singular desire to move on.

William turned to study the gallery of paintings on the white wall at the far side of the room. He'd been particularly taken with the work of Scottish artists. There was a group — an informal alliance he'd heard it described — of Elizabethan artists known as The Glasgow Boys. The painting he really aspired to owning hung in the city's Kelvingrove Art Gallery.

It was a melancholic scene of a Highland funeral where the all-male mourners stood plaintively around a coffin outside a remote Scottish croft house. Sir James Guthrie had painted it with snow on the ground and a lowering grey sky. The poignancy filled William with sadness, and yet he was so drawn to it.

But there were other lesser-known paintings by Guthrie, James Paterson and Edward Walton that he had managed to buy. They hadn't been cheap, but that had never been the point.

There were other works too; that he

took comfort from having around him, but these did not have a permanent home in his London apartment.

He went to the drinks cabinet and poured himself a large measure of eighteen-year-old Glenfiddich single malt and drank it down in a succession of quick gulps, and then poured another.

If he'd gone to the window and looked out along the road he might have recognized the car parked at the end of the square, and the driver who was watching his apartment. But his mind was in another place, so he hadn't crossed over to the window.

His eye strayed back to the shattered photo frame. It was still painful to remember the past.

William poured himself a third whisky and sat brooding over it. It had been a mistake to come back here. London was no refuge for him. There was only one place where he truly belonged now. He went through to the bedroom and started to throw clothes into a black leather case. He wasn't aware of the car down below, and the driver who still sat there . . . watching.

William slipped on a jacket, picked up the case and made his unsteady way out to the square. The car started and began to cruise slowly along behind him.

The driver would have to act soon, leaving it too long would mean the prey had entered busier roads, and that would make the task of killing him so much harder.

William had no idea what had made him stop suddenly and put the overnight bag he had so hurriedly packed down on the pavement. As he turned to glance back along the road, the driver hit the accelerator, jamming a foot to the floor. The car shot forward. William leapt aside as it mounted the pavement and tore past him. But he hadn't been quick enough jumping clear and the car caught him a glancing blow. As he crashed to the ground he'd had the merest impression of the driver's cold cruel eyes behind the dark glasses. And then the blackness enveloped him.

He hadn't heard the car screech away, and hadn't seen the woman's hands trembling on the steering wheel. Had she killed him? She hoped so. He was dangerous, a loose cannon that could destroy her at any time. She couldn't allow that to happen.

Even now the memory of him still had the power to send a chill down her spine. She hadn't planned that first meeting, hadn't appreciated the control being taken out of her hands. Even so, he hadn't recognized her; he hadn't been meant to. She'd worked hard enough over the years to change her appearance, her personality, and her voice. It had taken patience to work on modulating those tones, eradicating the harsh accent.

The only thing that hadn't altered was her thirst for vengeance.

Her thoughts slipped back again to that day when he'd walked into the room. She could see herself lifting her gaze, watching him. He'd looked up and caught her eye and gave a polite smile, but his scrutiny lingered and she thought she'd detected a slight narrowing of the eyes.

It had taken all of her self-control not to react to that look, but she'd taken comfort from the knowledge that he couldn't possibly have recognized her.

The name he'd given was not his own, but that hadn't been surprising. Many people under those circumstances created an alter ego for themselves. She knew that, and it hadn't been a worry. In fact it was perfect. Knowing his secret gave her even more power over him. He was like a lamb to the slaughter, and she would enjoy taking full advantage of that.

# 19

Loveday lay in bed listening to Sam's easy breathing. She had no idea why she was so concerned about Scobey being missing, except that he probably wasn't. The man had every right to take himself away for a few days without having the police prying into his privacy. But what if he was in trouble? What if he'd been murdered like Jamie? She shivered under the duvet and felt Sam's arm coming around her. She snuggled into him.

If Scobey still hadn't returned by the next day then Maya wouldn't be the only one to have serious fears.

Concentrating her thoughts on the mystery of Tom Scobey was an attempt to avoid more graphic things, but it clearly wasn't working because the image of those bones in the old burial site still kept racing through her mind. The skeleton had once been a woman, and Loveday had a strong feeling she'd been a young woman, perhaps no older than herself. She'd been a woman who was loved. She had the ring. Perhaps Sam's team could get some kind of lead from that? She remembered the inscription '*For precious secrets.*' The jeweller who engraved it would surely remember those words.

But how to find him? The ring could have been bought anywhere, perhaps not even in this country.

She sighed. Her thoughts were taking her round in circles. Solving these murders was not her responsibility yet she couldn't get them out of her head. She lifted the duvet and slipped out of bed, glancing back to make sure she hadn't disturbed Sam. He was still sleeping like a baby.

She moved to the window and drew the curtain aside. The bay looked so still and peaceful. There was no breeze to ruffle the surface of the water; even the gulls had not yet stirred from their sleep. She raised her arms and took a lazy stretch as she watched the streaks of golden light begin to seep across the sky. The first glint of sunshine caught one of the windows on

St Michael's Mount. Loveday smiled. It was going to be a lovely day.

★ ★ ★

It hadn't escaped Sam's notice that they had a second body at another of Cornwall's ancient sites. The skeleton burial was historic, but until Dr Bartholomew confirmed how long it had been there they needed to keep an open mind. Still, it seemed more than a coincidence. And he didn't like coincidences. No matter how unlikely it seemed these bodies must be connected.

He'd left before the traffic got too busy, but on lovely mornings like this there was no way to avoid the early morning sun. It sat at a low angle over the A30, dazzling drivers and causing them to snap down their visors. Sam reached into the pocket for his sunglasses and put them on.

It was one hazard Loveday was unlikely to face, as her journey into Truro was usually so much later than his. Sam fixed his eyes on the road ahead, but his mind was back at the cottage in Marazion.

Loveday had looked tired when he left her. That meant she hadn't slept well, even though she'd insisted that she had.

One of them worrying about these murders was quite enough, but then it hadn't been him who had discovered the skeleton.

Photos of the ring and the inscription would have been circulated to every jeweller in Cornwall by now. Unless DNA came up with something, it was the only clue they had. It might have no connection to Jamie Roscow's murder but they couldn't take any chances.

He reflected back on yesterday's visit with Will to Walter Allen. The man had been as arrogant as ever — until he was asked if Jamie had ever taken him to the fogou. He hadn't exactly panicked, but there had been something about that pause before answering that had made Sam suspicious.

In the end his story had sounded fairly convincing, but he'd be good at that. Making things up was the writer's stock in trade. And Walter Allen was clever enough at it to have made a fortune.

Sam had despatched DC Carter to have another word with the man. He would have preferred to do that himself again, but he couldn't be everywhere and he had to call in at the mortuary.

He'd read Walter's witness statement where he'd been asked to go into more detail about his association with Jamie, and what exactly he had done for his parents.

'Jamie was a friend. His parents had asked me to look out for him. I felt responsible,' he'd said.

Walter Allen's responses had definitely appeared cautious and Sam could think of only one reason for that. The man had something to hide

\* \* \*

Loveday nursed a mug of coffee standing by the kitchen door as she watched Sam's car heading off up the drive and turning right along the seafront. She felt ridiculously desolate as the Lexus disappeared from view.

Poor Sam. He seemed to be facing an

266

impossible task and there was nothing she could do to help him. She tried to imagine how the morning's briefing session would go. It was almost a week since they'd found Jamie's body, and as far as she knew they were no closer to finding his killer. If they couldn't do that then what chance did they have of discovering who killed this latest victim? All they had to go on was a skeleton and a ring.

Beyond the drive, Loveday could see that the tide was on the way out. Soon the beach would be busy with streams of tourists heading for the causeway to St Michael's Mount. It all looked so comfortingly normal compared to what was going on in Sam's and her lives.

She glanced across to where Cassie's Land Rover was normally parked. It wasn't there, not that she had time for cosy chats. She had something to do before going to the office. She slipped her mobile phone out of her pocket and punched in Merrick's number. It went on to answerphone.

'Hi, Merrick,' she said. 'Just letting you

know that I'm off to do an interview for the antiquities feature. I should be back around eleven. I'll keep in touch.'

She narrowed her eyes, staring back out across the bay. The sun was glinting off the water. It was a perfect May morning. She felt a sudden urge to join the people who would soon be walking across the beach. She could almost hear the sound of their voices drifting back to her, carefree, happy voices. The voices of people enjoying their time in Cornwall.

She let the phone drop back into her pocket and went back into the kitchen to rinse out her cup and stack it in the drainer. She locked up and went to her car, started the engine and set off in the direction of Carn Hendra.

'I thought I recognized you, my dear.' Lizzie Tangye puffed up behind Loveday as she made her way to the fogou half an hour later.

She wheeled round to stare at the newcomer. 'Mrs Tangye!'

Lizzie Tangye stopped and fished in her apron pocket for a hankie and proceeded to mop her brow.

'You wouldn't believe how popular this place has become since that poor lad's body was found. Morbid . . . that's what I call it. There's no accounting for some folk.'

The woman blew out her cheeks and rested her shoulder against the stone interior of the dark passage. 'You don't half walk at some pace, my love.'

'Did you want to speak to me, Mrs Tangye?'

'That I did. Look, I'm not trying to lay down any rules or anything, but this place does belong to you now, and somebody needs to be responsible for it.'

Loveday frowned. 'I'm sorry. What exactly is the problem?'

'I said, didn't I? You need to put this out of bounds or something . . . stop the public from wandering all over the place. My Clem wouldn't say nothing, but we've already had the potato crop trampled.' She pointed back towards the couple's farmhouse. 'And that corn is going to go the same way.'

Loveday stared out in the direction Mrs Tangye was indicating. She could see the damaged crops. It wasn't much, but she could see it becoming a problem if what the farmer's wife described escalated.

'I'd no idea. I'm so sorry. What can I do to help?'

She wasn't sure why she was taking the blame for this. It wasn't as though she'd sent out an open invitation to trespass on her land.

The woman placed a work-weary hand on her chest and sighed.

'Oh, pay no heed to me, my love; I needed somebody to moan at. I'm sorry it was you. I know it's not your fault.'

Loveday smiled. 'I can see how this would be annoying.' She nodded towards the damaged crops. 'I'm just not sure what I can do about it.'

'No, and nor do I, but the kettle's on the stove back in the kitchen. Maybe a cup of tea will help the both of us to think better.'

It wasn't an offer Loveday was about to turn down. She remembered the big friendly farmhouse kitchen, and Lizzie Tangye would undoubtedly be a source of much information.

'That's a great idea. Thank you.' She smiled, but the woman had already turned and was heading back to her farmhouse.

She kept up a continuous monologue of chat as she clumped ahead along the uneven track between the fields. Loveday was only half listening. She didn't really know what she was doing back here at the fogou.

She'd told Merrick she was interviewing someone. At least now that could be true, and there was no telling what she might learn from this woman.

She glanced back at the rubble in the middle of the field, knowing that this had once the home of her great-aunt Martha. There was no way she would ever be able to rebuild it. And if she did manage that . . . well, she wasn't likely to live out here on the remote clifftop. It wouldn't be practical.

And then there was the murder . . .

She sighed. Sam's investigation didn't seem to be progressing much.

'You're in luck, my love, it's my baking day and there's a tray of scones to be eaten,' Lizzie Tangye called back as they approached the farmhouse.

The battered red tractor was not in the yard. Loveday hoped it was a sign that the farmer was not at home.

Any discussion between her and Lizzie would definitely go better without Tangye.

'Slip off your jacket, my love, and sit yourself down,' the woman said as she ushered her visitor into her kitchen.

Loveday glanced around. A big battered brown kettle simmered on the stove. Her eyes rested on the tray of scones. Breakfast had been half a slice of toast. She could already feel her mouth watering.

'Can I do anything to help?' she asked.

But Lizzie shooed her to a chair. 'It'll only take a minute. You just rest yourself till it's ready.'

Loveday watched the woman glide happily around her kitchen, stretching up to remove mugs from their hooks and reaching into a cupboard for sugar.

The scones tasted as delicious as they had looked, and Loveday's finger caught a dribble of soft yellow farmhouse butter on her chin.

The woman watched her, smiling. 'I like a lass who knows how to enjoy her food.'

Loveday blushed, aware that she was already on her second scone. 'These are delicious,' she said, swallowing a mouthful of crumbs.

Lizzie Tangye glowed with pleasure at the compliment. 'Tangye takes it all for granted. I should go on strike. That's what I should do.'

'You spoil him.'

Lizzie indulged in one of her deep sighs. 'I do that all right.'

Loveday followed her gaze to the tiny window. The outline of Tangye's tractor could be seen moving slowly across the far field.

'That writer chap was back here, you know.' She nodded out towards the fogou. 'And if I'm any judge of character, he didn't want to be seen. He must have left his car parked way back down the lane before he went skulking around the field to the place.'

Loveday's ears perked up. 'What writer?' she asked, but she already knew who Lizzie was referring to.

'You know the one,' the farmer's wife went on. 'That one that writes them raunchy books.'

Loveday got up and went to the window to glance down the rutted track. Her Clio was there, but behind it the lane took a sharp turn to the left. Any vehicle parked further back would have been out of sight from the house.

'How did you know it was the writer? You can't see what might be parked further down the lane.'

Loveday swung round. The woman had got up; feet planted firmly apart, her arms folded. 'Did I say it was me that saw him?'

'Sorry . . . I thought — '

'It was Tangye that saw him.' She nodded out over the clifftop. 'Working in the far field out there, he was. The man was sneaking about around the edges of the field. Scurrying about like a rat he was. And then he disappeared into the fogou. And he had a torch. It was a dark murky day and Tangye could see the light inside the passage.'

She stopped for a breath.

'A bit weird if you ask me. I can just about understand why the thrill seekers would want to come here, but that poor dead young man was supposed to be his friend. Why would he come back?'

Loveday saw a shiver shake the woman's body.

'It's pure morbid if you ask me.'

But Loveday's mind had flown back to Walter Allen.

'How do you know they were friends?'

'I've seen them together.' She nodded out towards the fogou. 'Out there. They've been here before . . . the two of them.'

She pressed her lips together and gave a knowing nod. The implication the woman was making was clear.

There had been no suggestion that Jamie had been gay. Loveday thought back to her and Sam's last meeting with the writer. She was remembering the way the writer had looked at her when he thought she hadn't noticed. No. Walter Allen wasn't gay. Quite the opposite if she was any judge.

So what were they doing here at the fogou? And what was the writer doing returning to the place?

The possibility that Walter had killed Jamie after all filtered through her mind. He could have . . . why not?

But why would he? What possible reason could he have had for murdering Jamie Roscow?

She was still thinking about this long after she had thanked the farmer's wife for her tea and scones and was on her way back to Truro.

Some people might think it odd that she was there herself today. She wasn't quite sure why she'd gone to the fogou. But then she did own the site now, not that she had any clearer idea of what to do with it.

Lizzie Tangye's information about Walter Allen returning to the place had confirmed something she'd been considering. The solution to Jamie Roscow's murder was still somewhere out there in that fogou. They had to find it!

# 20

Loveday's mobile rang as she got back to her car. It was Sam.

'Fancy a sandwich in the pub later?' he suggested.

'Sounds great. What time?'

'Is one o'clock OK with you?'

'I'll look forward to it,' she smiled.

Her spirits had lifted as she drove to Truro.

Keri was on the phone as Loveday strolled into the office. She looked up, reaching for the diary and began scribbling an entry.

'Teo Grahl, that artist who makes sculptures out of driftwood has confirmed a time for his interview,' she said. 'Next Tuesday at ten. Is that OK?'

'Depends whether you're free or not,' Loveday said, holding her smile in check.

Keri stared at her. 'You want me to do the interview?' Her eyes sparkled. 'Are you sure?'

'Of course I'm sure. Take Mylor with you so we can get the photographs all done at the same time.' She thought Keri was about to bound around the desk and hug her.

'Will I get a byline?' Keri asked hopefully.

'Absolutely you will. I'll make sure of it.'

'Thank you, Loveday. I'll do a really good job. I promise.'

Loveday smiled back at her friend. She had no doubt about that. Keri had the makings of a good journalist. She deserved her chance.

The next two hours were spent industriously tapping the research details she had so far compiled on Cornwall's ancient relics into her computer. It was coming together nicely.

When she glanced at the clock it was ten to one. Keri had already gone for lunch. She glanced up at Merrick's office, but he was deep in conversation on the phone.

The thought of seeing Sam made her feel ridiculously light-hearted as she hurried along Lemon Street and into Boscawen Street to the pub. Sam was already standing at the bar.

'What are you having, Loveday?' He had a pint of Doom Bar in front of him.

'Half cider please, and a cheese and chutney sandwich.'

'Make that two sandwiches.' Sam nodded to the barman, who had already started to pour Loveday's cider.

Their favourite table by the window was free, so she settled into it. Sam joined her, a glass in each hand.

He tilted his head, studying her as he sat down. 'You look a lot more cheerful than when I left this morning. I was worried about you.'

She reached across the table and touched his hand. 'I quite like you worrying about me, Sam, but there's no need. I'm fine.'

He went on looking at her and then gave a solemn nod. 'Well, no more finding bodies, eh?'

'I'll try.' She laughed back.

Sam was right, she had been a bit depressed that morning, but her spirits were up now. She had a thought she wanted to run past him.

'Do you suppose Jamie could have been blackmailing Walter Allen?' she asked.

'Where did that come from?'

Loveday shrugged. 'It was something Mrs Tangye said today.'

Sam's eyebrows shot up.

'You were out there today. Why?'

Loveday shot him a warning look.

'I do own that site now. Remember?'

'Yes . . . but — '

'No buts, Sam. I went to have another look at the place. Lizzie Tangye spotted my car and made it her business to find out what I was doing there.'

She gave him a half smile. 'She'd be good on your team. She'd sort that Amanda out for you.'

Sam ignored the remark about his fiery DC. 'So what exactly did Mrs Tangye tell you?' He was very aware that he had not shared with her Clem Tangye's disclosure of his affair with Loveday's aunt. He'd have to choose his time for that.

He concentrated instead on listening

quietly as she recounted her meeting with the old farmer's wife. Sam made no attempt to interrupt her, and remained silent for several minutes after she'd finished.

Loveday drained her glass, watching him.

Sam frowned. Lizzie Tangye had not told them she knew Jamie and Walter Allen had been friends. She'd only mentioned the young couple that had visited the fogou before Jamie's body was discovered — the couple they now knew to have been Jamie and Maya. So what was she up to? First her husband finds the body in the fogou and doesn't report it, and now this.

'Well?' Loveday scowled at him. 'Am I right? Was Jamie blackmailing Walter Allen?'

Sam sat back in his chair and rubbed his chin. He was still wondering about Lizzie Tangye. Loveday repeated the question.

Sam shook his head. He'd only now realised what she was saying. 'I doubt it,' he said. 'Jamie doesn't strike me as the blackmailing type.'

'There's a type?'

'You know what I mean.'

She did. Sneaky was a word that came to mind. No one she spoke to gave the impression that Jamie had been sneaky. She tried to remember how Ben Poldavy had described him. He'd been a friend, enough of a friend to worry about when he disappeared.

And then there was Maya. But she had adored Jamie.

Loveday flicked her mind back to Walter Allen. Now there was a man who was definitely sneaky. Could Jamie really have been blackmailing him? More likely the other way round, but then Jamie was the one who had got himself killed, so somebody hadn't liked him. But why?

She let her mind dwell on this for a moment. What could Jamie possibly have done to get himself murdered?

Maybe he hadn't been blackmailing anyone. Maybe he just knew someone's secrets. If the secret was damaging enough, and the person involved couldn't risk it being discovered, would that be sufficient reason for murder?

'OK,' Sam said, squinting at her as he repositioned a beer mat under his glass. 'I hardly dare to ask what's going on in your head.'

'I was thinking about Jamie actually. Do you think he could have known somebody's secret and that's what got him killed?'

'What kind of secret?'

Loveday shrugged. 'Don't know. That's as far as I got.'

Sam settled back in his chair and took a slow swig of ale. His mind went back to all the people who knew Jamie.

Ben had been the first to mention him, but Sam had long ago ruled him out as a suspect. What about Jamie's parents? Charles and Sarah Roscow were a wealthy couple whose son hadn't come up to their expectations. No. He corrected that. It had been *her* expectations that Jamie hadn't met. Had Sarah been ashamed of Jamie? She had certainly been exasperated by his behaviour . . . maybe even furious that he refused to join their business.

Had Jamie known family secrets so

shocking that he had to be silenced?

Sam weighed up the possibilities that either Sarah or Charles had killed their son. But then they were out of the country when Jamie died. He frowned. They *had* been out of the country, hadn't they? He had told Amanda to check and she hadn't got back to him. The question would go on his list of priorities for the morning briefing.

And what about Walter Allen? Sarah had admitted getting him to spy on Jamie. A thought struck him. If Walter was such a good friend of Jamie's parents then Jamie would have already known him. So he must also have known either his mum or dad would have asked the writer to check up on him.

And then there was Lizzie and Clem Tangye. Had they really known Jamie? They were definitely in line for another visit.

Technically they were all still in the frame for Jamie's murder, but he kept coming back to Walter Allen. He was certain that the man was more involved than he was admitting. But had he killed

Jamie? They needed to look at him again.

'I'll tell you a man who has secrets.' Loveday's voice cut into his thoughts, bringing him back into the room.

'Tom Scobey,' she said. 'Now there's a man of mystery if ever I met one. And now he's disappeared . . . ' She looked across at Sam. 'So what d'you reckon all that's about?'

Sam drained the last of his beer and put the empty glass back on the table. He leaned back, stretching his long legs and crossing them at the ankles before shrugging. He hadn't a clue. Finding the missing man was high on his team's priorities, but so far all their enquiries had drawn a blank. Scobey was proving a difficult character to pin down. He appeared not to have an insurance number, and they hadn't been able to track down any medical history.

They had discovered, through chasing down an estate agent, that he owned his cottage in Karrek, rather than rented it, which confirmed that he really did have money. But how had he come by it?

Loveday watched Sam chew his lip and

smiled to herself. She knew he was thinking over what she'd said.

They had been about to leave when Sam reached into his jacket pocket and took out a photograph. He handed it to Loveday.

'You won't have had much chance to look at this when you found it, but what about now? Does the ring look familiar?'

She studied the photo. The picture of the ring and a separate one of the inscription had been copied onto the same picture.

'If it's a diamond then it will be worth a fortune, but I'm guessing it's not,' she said.

Sam shook his head. 'Zircon — the poor man's diamond.'

'Can I keep this, Sam?' she asked.

He frowned. 'I'm not sure why you would want to, but it's fine. You can hang onto it.'

\* \* \*

Loveday's phone rang as she walked back to the office. She smiled, reaching into her pocket for it thinking it was Sam again, but it was Keri.

'Sorry to interrupt your lunch, Loveday, but I thought you'd want to know that Maya has just come into the office looking for you.'

'I'm almost there now. Can you make my excuses to Merrick?'

'No problem,' Keri told her.

Emily West, the magazine's young blonde receptionist, looked up and smiled when she saw Loveday. She glanced towards the young woman pacing the restricted front office area, and Loveday nodded.

'Maya! How are you?'

Maya moved towards her. 'Any chance we could step outside for a few minutes?'

Loveday thought of the mountain of work that awaited her upstairs, but she smiled. 'Let's have a stroll. We can talk as we walk.'

It was two o'clock and Lemon Street was busy. Loveday pitied the frustrated drivers she could see cruising around in search of parking places.

'I'm guessing this is about Jamie?'

Loveday said as they crossed the road and strolled towards the piazza on Lemon Quay.

Maya stopped and turned to face her. 'Look, I may have this all wrong, and I don't want to point the finger at anybody, but . . . ' She bit her lip, wondering how to say what she had to without it sounding ridiculous.

'Go on,' Loveday encouraged.

'I think Jamie had something on Walter.'

'You mean Jamie was blackmailing Walter?'

Maya shook her head. 'Jamie would never stoop to that kind of thing, but he liked to know where he stood with people. He didn't like secrets.'

Loveday kept silent, waiting for her to continue.

She did. 'He discovered something Walter didn't want him to know.'

'Like what?'

'Something about his books I think. He said it was best if I wasn't involved. He didn't trust Walter.'

'Did you trust him, Maya?'

The girl's shoulders rose in a shrug. 'I didn't know him . . . well, not like Jamie did. He was some kind of friend of the family.'

'Some kind of friend?'

'Put it this way. He was no friend of Jamie's. He certainly didn't trust the man.' She paused, meeting Loveday's eyes. 'I know I've mentioned this to you before, but maybe I didn't put it strongly enough. Walter wasn't just asking questions about Jamie. He was spying on him. Can you imagine that? Spying!'

'But why?' Loveday's brow wrinkled into a questioning frown. She wondered if Sam knew about this.

'Have you told the police about this, Maya?'

'I've only now worked it out, and I could be wrong but I think it has something to do with Jamie's parents. That's all I know, except that Jamie was pretty mad. The last thing he wanted was for his parents to find out where he was, but they always did.

'They hated the idea of Jamie having any life of his own. They didn't know their own son. They knew how much he detested the idea of going into their business and yet they kept pushing him.'

Loveday saw a tear glisten in Maya's eye and watched it spill over onto the girl's cheek. She stopped herself leaning forward to comfort her, sensing it wasn't what the girl wanted.

'This is all their fault,' Maya said, her voice shaking with emotion. 'Why could they not have left him alone?'

There was an empty table at the cafe in the piazza. A teenage lad in jeans and navy tee shirt was clearing tables and straightening chairs. He gave them no more than a cursory glance as they sat down.

'Can we have two coffees, please?' Loveday called to him.

He looked up and gave a distracted nod. He'd been miles away.

Maya had regained her composure by the time she turned back to her. 'Sorry about that,' she said, tucking the tissue she had been using into her jacket pocket. 'I thought I was all cried out.'

Loveday smiled and reached for Maya's

hand. 'Don't be so hard on yourself. There's nothing wrong with a good cry.'

Their coffee arrived and for a few moments they sat in silence, sipping it. Maya was looking thoughtful.

'I've given up my little flat in Helston, and I have no real right to stay on in Jamie's boat. Even Scobey has deserted me. There's nothing left for me in Cornwall.'

'So you haven't heard any more from Scobey?'

'No. He's gone now.' Loveday could hear the hurt in her voice as she said, 'And he never even said goodbye.'

'Well, doesn't that tell you he means to come back?'

'I don't know. I just feel so miserable and sick all the time. I'm losing all the people I cared about.'

'Tell you what. Why don't I come down to Karrek later today and we could pay another visit to Scobey's cottage. Maybe he's left a clue there about where he's gone. Something the police didn't find. Surely it's worth one more try?'

'If you like,' Maya said, 'but I think it will be a waste of time.'

# 21

It was just after five when Loveday drove into Karrek. Maya was waiting for her by the boat and they walked together up to Scobey's place.

'The police have put a padlock on the door,' Maya said, going round to the back of the cottage. 'And the broken window's been boarded up.' She gave the padlock a shake. 'I feel guilty. What if Scobey comes back? He'll be horrified to know the police had tramped all over his place.'

'Well, at least we would know he'd come back,' Loveday said.

'How do you work that out?'

'Wouldn't he go down to the pub or somewhere demanding to know who'd put the padlock on his back door?'

Maya shook her head. 'You don't know Scobey. He wouldn't see this as anyone else's business.'

Loveday frowned. She could understand someone choosing to protect his privacy, but surely that would be taking things too far, especially if he needed help?

Maya was already moving away. 'I'll take a look around,' she said, picking her way through the long grass and weeds.

Loveday walked the length of the front of the building. In other circumstances the traditional Cornish cottage could have been a desirable residence, especially in this secluded spot but the sad, derelict appearance did it no favours. It was less than half a mile from the village but there was a brooding sense of isolation about the place.

She wondered if this was why Scobey had bought it.

She didn't see the figure emerge from his hiding place in the bushes, or hear his silent approach until a twig snapped under his foot.

Loveday spun round and caught her breath. Penetrating grey eyes stared angrily into hers.

'What exactly are you doing here?' he growled.

Loveday's hand flew to her heart. 'Mr

Scobey! You startled me.'

'And your presence here startles me. What are you doing?'

Loveday swallowed, snatching time to regain her composure. The man's appearance was very different from the last time she saw him. The faded jeans and scruffy waistcoat had gone. In their place were fawn needle cord trousers and an expensive looking red striped shirt under a tan swede jacket. His dark, grey streaked hair looked freshly washed and had been caught back in a ponytail. 'We were looking for you,' she said.

'We?' Scobey frowned, his eyes searching all around.

'Maya and I,' Loveday explained. She called out Maya's name and the girl appeared from the side of the cottage. Her face broke into a huge grin when she spotted Scobey and ran at him, arms outstretched.

'Scobey!'

The man caught her and drew her into a hug. 'I should leave more often if this is the kind of reception I get when I come back.'

'Where have you been?' Maya drew back. She was studying the expensive clothes. 'We've been so worried.'

'We?' Scobey gave her a disbelieving smile.

'Loveday and I.' She spun round to Loveday. 'Tell him.'

Loveday swallowed. 'We've been looking for you, Mr Scobey. Have you been inside the cottage yet?'

Scobey frowned. 'Not yet. Is there something I should know?'

'You've been burgled,' Maya said quickly. 'Someone got in through the back window. I'm afraid your computer's gone.' She bit her bottom lip. 'And two of your paintings.'

A pained expression came into Tom Scobey's eyes. 'Not the Lowry and the Stanhope Forbes?'

Maya nodded. 'I'm afraid so, but the police are out looking for whoever did it. I'm sure you'll get everything back.'

Scobey looked at Loveday. 'Is that what you think too?'

'The police will do everything they can to recover your property.' It was then that she noticed the bruise on the side of his face. Maya saw it at the same time and reached out for him.

'You're hurt,' she said.

But Scobey brushed her hand away. 'It's just a scratch. I bumped into a door. Stupid of me.'

Maya didn't look any more convinced than Loveday. The man before her wasn't the Scobey she knew. Where had the expensive clothes come from? His appearance was so different. She had a feeling he wasn't intending to stick around. They followed him round to the back of the cottage.

'You haven't yet told us why you left,' she said.

'I had to go away. There was business that needed attending to.'

'You should have told me. I kept checking in case you'd come back. We were horrified when we discovered you'd been burgled.'

Scobey's eyes slid to the padlock. 'I see you've been looking after my interests.'

'Not me. The police put it there. I think they have been trying to find you as well.'

Scobey's eyebrows came together in a frown. 'What do the police want with me?' His voice was gruff.

'Well, there's the little matter of that burglary, and they're still investigating Jamie's murder,' Loveday said gently. 'I expect they need your help.'

'I've already spoken to the police. I know nothing about what happened to Jamie.'

Loveday was remembering the man's reaction when she and Sam broke the news to him and Maya on the boat that day. The look of shock on his face had been unmistakeable. But there had been more. There had been anger . . . much anger. He was still looking angry.

She nodded towards the cottage. 'I don't suppose you have any tea in there?'

Scobey's frown deepened and Loveday waited for him to tell them to go away when Maya chipped in, 'Yes, let's go inside. I think you owe us an explanation.'

Scobey sighed, placing a hand on the girl's shoulder. 'Maybe I can spare you five minutes.'

The milk in the fridge had gone off, so

it was cups of black tea that Loveday put before the two others.

Scobey stared down at the table. 'I don't know where to start.' He was still trying to decide if he should tell them the truth.

'You could explain why you left the village so suddenly,' Loveday said.

'And if you left a letter for me at the pub,' Maya chipped in.

Scobey's head came up. 'Letter? I didn't leave a letter. What did this letter say?'

Maya told him.

The light that came into his eyes told Loveday that he knew, or suspected, who *had* left it there. He grimaced. 'It's as I said before. I had business in London. I have a flat there. There's a cleaner who goes in from time to time, but I need to keep an eye on things myself.'

Loveday could understand why. If he'd kept two such valuable paintings in this rundown, insecure cottage, what must his London art collection be like, for she was sure he would have one.

'I didn't realize you had property in

London. Jamie never told me,' Maya said.

Loveday saw the man's eyes cloud with sadness. 'Jamie didn't know,' he said.

Was he regretting he hadn't told his friend about his other life, his more prosperous life? Something was going on. She couldn't quite put her finger on it, but it would come to her eventually.

'And there's something else I didn't tell Jamie — or you, Maya.'

They both looked at him.

'My name isn't Scobey. It's William Bentley. I came to Cornwall and gave myself a new identity to get out of the London rat race.'

Maya's mouth fell open. 'You reinvented yourself? But Jamie and I were your friends, why didn't you tell us?'

Scobey gave a weary shrug. 'I've no idea. I suppose I thought I was protecting my life down here. I should have trusted you both.'

'It still doesn't explain that letter,' Maya said. 'Why would anyone do that?'

But Loveday already knew. Whoever wrote the letter knew about Scobey's little trip to London, perhaps they had even followed him there. Had they attempted to harm him? The bruise on his face still concerned her, for he almost certainly hadn't got it from walking into a door.

Another thing was puzzling her. If this mystery person really had followed Scobey then they must have been watching him beforehand. And if they had left the village at the same time, then they couldn't have left the note. There was only one explanation Loveday could think of. Scobey's mystery stalker had an accomplice.

The ringing of her phone startled all three of them. She fumbled for it in her pocket, but as she drew it out it had stopped ringing. A missed call. But the photograph of the ring that Sam had given her came out with it and landed on the floor.

Scobey bent down to pick it up. Loveday saw him frown as he gazed at the picture.

'Do you recognize this ring, Mr Scobey?'

'I'm not sure,' he said slowly. 'It was a long time ago.'

A quiver of anticipation ran through her. 'It could be important. Please try to remember.'

'It looks like the ring Eva used to wear.'

'Eva?' Loveday questioned. Her excitement mounting.

'Eva Penney. She was the barmaid at the Badgers when I first came here. She moved to Australia.'

Maya came round from the other side of the kitchen table and looked at the photograph. 'It's just an ordinary ring. What's so special about it?'

'Yes, Mr Scobey. Why do you think you recognize it?'

'Because Eva thought it was a diamond. Her boyfriend had given it to her. She thought it was worth a fortune.'

'But you didn't think so?' Loveday said.

'It was a zircon, but I didn't tell Eva that. She was happy to believe she was wearing a fortune on her finger. I wasn't about to burst her bubble.'

'Who was her boyfriend? Was he a local man?'

'If he was she kept it very quiet. I got the impression he was married.'

Loveday was trying to keep her growing excitement in check. She said, 'You mentioned that Eva went to Australia. Did they both go?'

'Not at first, she went out there on her own. She told me her boyfriend would be following once he had dealt with his business in Cornwall.'

'And did anyone hear from Eva after she went abroad?' Loveday asked.

'Only the postcard. She sent a postcard from Sydney saying what a great time they were having over there. It was behind the bar in the pub for months.'

Loveday's mounting eagerness took a slump with his last sentence. If Eva was in Australia then the body in the barrow couldn't be her — or it was a different ring. But whatever it was, Sam had to know about this. And he had to know that Tom Scobey was back.

She excused herself and went outside to call him.

'I thought you should know, Sam,' she said after she had related Scobey's story.

'Thanks, Loveday,' he said. 'I definitely want a word with that man. You can go home now and leave this to me.'

Loveday gave an annoyed pout. She didn't like being dismissed. 'But don't you want me to stay here and keep an eye on him? What if Scobey runs off again, which he might do if I don't stay with him.'

She could almost hear Sam thinking. 'At the very least we can all have a drink together in the pub,' she coaxed.

He sighed. 'This business has upset you enough, Loveday. I don't want you getting in any deeper.'

'It would help Maya if I stay. She's finding all this much more upsetting than I am. She's lost her boyfriend after all.'

A pause, and then Sam said, 'OK, but I do all the talking. Is that agreed?'

'It's fine by me, Sam,' Loveday said, smiling as she clicked off the call.

She stared at the phone for a few seconds more. Something had just struck her. She called up the Photos app and began to click through it until she found what she was looking for. It was the picture she took of Jamie's painting. It would be better to examine it on the computer where she could see more detail, but for the moment she would have to make do with what she had.

She narrowed her eyes at the image and zoomed in on Walter Allen's figure at the end of the bar. She had thought he'd had a funny look in his eyes, but now she realized he had been looking at something behind the bar.

It was a tiny blob of colour. Could it be a postcard? Could it be a postcard from Eva?

# 22

Sam was first to arrive in the CID room. He glanced across to the Murder Wall, fixing his stare on Walter Allen's face. Could Loveday be right? Could he have known about that barrow?

He'd called up at his house last night in Karrek but he wasn't home. Tom Scobey's suggestion that the ring was similar to one owned by Eva Penney was confirmed by the landlord of the Badger Inn.

Sam had asked if he'd kept Eva's postcard, but he hadn't. It had been two years since Eva left, Seth Vingoe reminded Sam.

The man hadn't known any more than Scobey who the barmaid's boyfriend was, and he didn't know of any male who had left the village around that time.

He was still mulling over the possibilities as the briefing room gradually filled.

'We need to have another word with

our author friend out at Karrek,' Sam told Amanda, as she settled herself at the table.

'Yes, boss. Will you be coming?'

Sam shook his head. 'Show him the photograph of the ring and watch his reaction. We need to know how well acquainted he was with Eva Penney the barmaid.'

Amanda nodded. She felt that at last she was being trusted with a job she could get her teeth into.

'And you haven't yet reported back on your checks into the Roscows whereabouts at the time of their son's murder,' Sam said.

Amanda coloured. She had forgotten all about that, but she could hardly say so. She swallowed. 'Sorry, boss. I thought I'd left a note on your desk. Everything checks out. The couple were definitely not in Cornwall around then. They're out of the frame.'

Sam knew he should take the detective to task for her slipshod work, but then maybe he should have asked her for an update sooner. And he had kept her busy out at Carn Hendra. If she was to be believed, she'd put Lizzie Tangye through the mill with questions about why she hadn't told them she'd seen Jamie with Walter Allen. Her story was that she hadn't realized it was important. She didn't know who Jamie was until the publicity that followed his murder. It was only when she saw his picture in the local newspaper that she realized it was the same young man who had called with the girl asking permission to visit the fogou. Her story made sense, and Sam was inclined to believe it.

The rest of the team had started to arrive. Sam positioned himself in front of the wall and was about to brief his detectives on the latest information on Tom Scobey when the door opened and DC Malcolm Carter rushed in.

'Sorry, boss, but we have another body — out Buryan way at the Merry Maidens.'

Sam's heart sank — another historic site. This one was a stone circle off the B3315 Newlyn to Treen road. It was a popular site with tourists because the monument was so close to the road.

'When was this?' he snapped. It was the last thing they needed.

'A few minutes ago. A young couple on their way to walk the coastal path called it in. The local plods are with them now.'

'Tell them to tape off the site as best they can,' Sam instructed. 'We don't want any more trippers tramping all over it. And get Dr Bartholomew out there, but hold off calling out the rest of the troops until I give the word.' He was remembering the lectures he'd had from the cash-conscious Superintendent Harry Bolger about staying within budgets.

'Right, boss,' Malcolm said, already reaching for his phone.

'Will and Amanda, you two come with me.'

A convoy of CID vehicles sped out of the car park and through the busy city streets towards the A30.

'Another ancient site,' Will said, frowning as they joined the roundabout with Amanda Fox following in the car behind. 'It's beginning to look like we have a serial killer.'

'Let's see what we have here before we jump to conclusions,' Sam said. 'We don't know that our body is even suspicious yet. We can't rule out natural causes until we see it.'

But the phrase serial killer was already tearing around Sam's head, and he wasn't enjoying the possibility one bit.

The patrol car from Penzance was parked in the lay-by next to the stile that gave access to the field where the stone circle was. A young PC was waiting by his vehicle for them. They all piled out of the cars and ducked under the tapes.

More police vehicles screeched up behind them.

'You stay here, Constable,' Sam ordered, as Amanda handed him one of the white scene suits she'd taken from the boot of her car. 'And wave on any curious sightseers. Let's keep this as low key as possible for the moment.'

He was first to scramble over the high steps of the stile and stride out across the field. Will and Amanda were close behind.

Sam presumed the young couple he could see standing outside the stone circle with another uniformed officer were the ones Malcolm had mentioned. The scene tape had been wound slalom fashion between the stones but it had already slipped to the ground.

He beckoned the officer aside. 'You've checked the vital signs?'

'The chap's dead, sir,' the officer said flatly. 'And I'd say he's been a goner for some hours, probably some time last night.'

He saw Sam's eyebrow arch and cleared his throat, embarrassed at giving a senior officer information that should be down to the police pathologist.'

'Sorry, sir. I just meant . . . '

'It's fine, Constable,' Sam said, 'you've done all the right things.'

He glanced across at the fully clothed body sprawled in the centre of the circle, frowning as he approached it. It wasn't looking good. He kept his distance as he walked around the scene.

The body was face down on the rough grass. The back of the victim's head was covered in blood, presumably resulting from the deep wound Sam could clearly see. He sighed. Not a heart attack then!

He nodded to Will to get the forensic team out. 'And tell Malcolm we'll need him too.'

'I'm on it, boss,' Will said, his mobile phone already at his ear.

Amanda was despatched to take statements from the two young people who found the body.

Sam stared at the corpse. He could hear the purr of the Home Office pathologist's big green BMW pulling up on the far side of the hedge. He couldn't see the dead man's face but he was pretty sure he knew who he was.

He stood back as Dr Bartholomew puffed up beside him. He was already in his scene suit. 'Not another one,' he commented grimly, looking down at the body as he unpacked his things.

He and Will watched as the pathologist made his preliminary examination while they waited for the arrival of the police photographer.

It was some minutes before Danny Morrison turned up. Sam used the time to walk around the circle, scanning the site for any piece of potential evidence. He saw nothing significant, but if the evidence was there then Danny's eagle eye would spot and photograph it.

Danny's camera clicked continuously as Dr Bartholomew acknowledged his nod to turn the body.

Will couldn't hide his shock as it was rolled over and the dead grey eyes of Walter Allen stared up at them.

Sam hid a groan. Allen had been their chief suspect for the murders of Jamie and Eva Penney. The fact that he had now become a murder victim himself didn't let him off the hook for those two killings, but it did complicate things. They would have to rethink the whole case.

Bartholomew was kneeling by the body, inserting a thermometer into it. He shook down the mercury and squinted at the reading. 'Can't be definite until I get him on the slab but it looks like he's been dead for some hours. Rigor mortis is already setting in.'

He glanced up at Sam. 'I can't confirm that he died of that head wound, but I'd be surprised if it wasn't the case.'

'I don't suppose you can suggest a likely weapon?' But he already knew what the man was going to say. He just wanted his suspicious confirmed.

'Look around you,' Bartholomew said, indicating the scattering of large stones. 'You might be lucky enough to find the murder weapon right here.' He gave a sarcastic smile. 'It'll be the one with the blood.'

Sam tried to stop his eyes rolling heavenwards. 'I'm sure my team will be grateful for your insight.'

The professor struggled up to his feet and stretched. 'You seem to be attracting bodies like confetti, Inspector. Maybe you should think about taking a holiday. Take those two great kids of yours — and the delectable Miss Ross, of course — away somewhere warm.'

'Believe me, Robert,' Sam said. 'I'd be grateful to stay out of the heat right now. And yes, I had noticed the increasing body count.'

'Try to keep it down to the three, Sam, there's a good chap.' Dr Bartholomew grimaced. 'I'm getting too old for all this.'

Sam put a hand on his old friend's

shoulder. 'Take care of yourself old man. Maybe you're the one who needs a holiday.'

The pathologist reached down for his expensive brown leather bag and nodded. 'It's on the agenda,' he said as he turned and walked away from the scene.

A cavalcade of vehicles had started to arrive, and the site was rapidly filling with members of the forensic team.

Amanda came across to Sam. 'Can the walkers go now, boss? They're in Cornwall on holiday but I have their local and home addresses.'

'Did they give us anything helpful?'

Amanda made a face. 'Sorry. They spotted the body as they passed the stones. They assured me they didn't go anywhere near it, just used the lad's mobile to make a 999 call.'

'Yeah, let them go. No need to spoil their holiday any more than we have to. Malcolm's on his way. Could you two ask around the neighbourhood to see if anyone noticed anything suspicious?'

He noted the young detective's look of despair. 'I know . . . I know. We don't exactly have a street of possible witnesses on tap, but check around local farms, holiday cottages, etc.

'I don't think our man was killed somewhere else and his body brought here. Why go to all that trouble? It would make more sense if he and his killer came here together. Somebody may have seen a car in the lay-by late last night.'

Amanda's expression told him how unlikely she thought that idea was in such a remote spot, but she wasn't in a position to object, and they didn't exactly have a lot of options.

He beckoned Will across. 'We need to see the grieving widow, even if that means driving to London.'

Will groaned. 'Well, let's pray she's here in Cornwall. A five hour drive on the M4 isn't my idea of fun.'

Sam smiled, but he wasn't relishing that drive either.

★   ★   ★

Loveday sat at her desk staring at the blank computer screen. She wasn't in a mood for working. Reaching into her bag she took out her reporters' notebook and a pen. She had no idea how it would help to make a list of all the people connected to the two murders, but it gave her something to do.

The list grew longer as she added name after name. She was looking for someone who might have a connection to Eva. All the regulars at the Badger Inn would have known her. She scrolled down the list, ticking off names — Walter Allen, Tom Scobey, the pub landlord, Seth Vingoe. She discounted Jamie and Maya since they hadn't arrived in the village until after Eva had gone.

Two names jumped out at her — Walter Allen and Tom Scobey. What did she know about them? There was something a bit strange about both of them.

Her mind went back to the look Allen had given her when she and Sam visited his place. There had been no mistaking its meaning. Walter Allen fancied himself as a ladies' man.

Had he looked at Eva like that? Had he

taken it further? It was a possibility.

She sipped the last of her coffee, deep in thought. Both victims had been found at ancient Cornish relics. Other than that there was nothing to connect them . . . except for the Karrek pub — and its customers Allen and Scobey.

Loveday frowned. If the skeleton in the barrow was Eva she was no closer to knowing who had killed her, or why they would take her body all the way out to that remote site on the Lizard? And how would anyone have even known the old barrow was there when at the time of the woman's death the local archaeological team had no idea about it?

★   ★   ★

It was Elizabeth Callington herself who appeared when Sam rapped on the door of Hillcrest.

'Walter's not here,' she said curtly. 'He's gone up to London on business.'

Sam smiled. 'It's you we've come to see. Ms Callington. May we come in?'

She gave the detectives an irritated

317

frown but stepped aside for them to pass her.

There was no whiff of the expensive perfume Sam had detected on the previous occasion he'd met her, and to his mind the woman's make-up hadn't been applied with the same detailed care as before.

He noted the two large cream leather cases in the hall.

She led them into the sitting room where even the view of the river failed to relieve the expensive gloom of the wood panelled walls.

Sam waited until they were settled. 'When did Mr Allen leave for London?'

Elizabeth crossed the room to take a cigarette from a silver box on the mantelpiece. 'Early yesterday morning,' she said crisply. 'Why do you want to know?'

But Sam wasn't ready to give that away quite yet. He wasn't at all sure of this woman.

'What was his business in London?'

'He had an appointment with his tailor in Savile Row. He was having a couple of new suits made up.' She lit the cigarette from a heavy gold-coloured table lighter and clattered it back onto the coffee table. 'Look. What's this all about?'

Sam glanced across to Will.

'When did you last hear from your husband, Ms Callington?' Will asked.

They both watched her carefully as she answered.

'When he left here yesterday,' she snapped. 'We are not in each other's pockets, you know.'

Sam went to the window and stood with his back to it. 'We have some bad news for you, Ms Callington. A body was discovered this morning. We believe it to be your husband. I'm so sorry.'

Elizabeth Callington's chin tilted up and she gave them an icy stare. 'What are you talking about? Walter is in London. I'll call the house now if you like.'

She crossed the room, snatched up a phone and punched in the numbers. Her hands were shaking.

'Leanne? It's me. Let me speak to Mr Allen.'

They watched her swallow and stare at the phone.

She looked up at them. 'He's not there.'

The detectives were silent, waiting for a reaction from the woman. They had after all just told her that her husband was dead.

Elizabeth Callington shook her head. 'I don't understand. I want to see this body. It can't possibly be Walter.'

Sam checked his watch. It was unlikely that the body had yet been moved to the mortuary. 'It might take a while to arrange, but you can most certainly do that. Either DS Tregellis or myself will collect you.'

Sam had an uneasy feeling as they drove away from the house. It wasn't anything he could put his finger on, but there was something.

'What did you think of that reaction?' he asked Will.

His sergeant's eyes never moved from the road ahead. 'She's a cool one, that's for sure, but then I never got the impression that she and Allen were a close couple.'

'Neither did I,' Sam said. 'But she was

his wife, there should have been some show of emotion.'

He was still thinking about that as he drove back to Marazion that evening.

# 23

Loveday had been itching all day to learn more about the discovery of the body in the stone circle. Who was it? Had he been murdered? How had he been killed? Who had Sam interviewed?

She had been tempted to drive out to the scene but she knew Sam would have been furious with her if she'd done that. The short news bulletin on the radio had only mentioned the discovery of a body and that police were treating it as suspicious. She could have phoned Sam and asked him outright, but he was hardly likely to tell her.

She sat on the rickety wooden bench in front of her cottage window and stared out over Mounts Bay. It had turned six and Marazion's seafront was still busy with promenading visitors. She sipped at her tea, but it had gone cold. She was about to go and exchange it for a glass of wine when Sam's car turned into the drive.

She forced herself to stay cool. She wouldn't ask. She would wait until he told her. She went to meet him, standing on tiptoes to plant a kiss on his cheek.

'Busy day?'

Sam screwed up his face. 'You could say that.'

'You know you can tell me anything, and it won't go any further,' Loveday said, pouring the remains of the Chardonnay bottle into another glass for Sam, and handed it to him.

He shook his head, laughing. 'I was wondering how many seconds it would be before you asked.'

'Asked?' Loveday said innocently. 'Asked about what?'

'About the body we found.'

She took his hand and all but dragged him into the sitting room and pushed him into a chair. 'Don't move. I'll fetch my glass and you can tell me all about it.'

She listened with wide-eyed intent as Sam talked.

'Walter Allen? It was Walter Allen's body?' She hadn't been expecting that.

'But wasn't he your prime suspect?'

'Just because he got himself bumped off doesn't mean he didn't do the other two killings.'

Loveday considered that. 'If you're looking for motive then Jamie's parents must be in the frame. Maybe they discovered that Walter killed their son and they took their revenge.'

'That thought hadn't escaped us, which is why we checked it out. They weren't in the country at the time,' Sam said.

Loveday blushed. 'Of course not, but who else is there?'

Sam shrugged. 'Take your pick. Walter Allen upset a lot of people. He was not the most appealing of characters.'

Loveday had only met the man that once when she'd gone with Sam to his house in Karrek. Maya didn't like him, but she wasn't capable of hurting a fly, let alone killing another human being. What about Scobey? He was a bit of a mystery — and he *was* back in the area.

'Fancy a takeaway?' Sam asked, jolting her out of her musings. 'I haven't eaten all day.'

She jumped up. 'There's a lasagne in

the freezer, and plenty of salad stuff in the fridge. It will only take half an hour.'

'Fine by me,' Sam said. He wasn't fancying standing in a queue at the local fish and chip shop.

They ate their supper from trays on their knees and didn't return to the subject of Walter Allen's murder until they had cleaned their plates and had mugs of hot coffee in their hands.

'So how do you think he got to the stones?' Loveday asked. 'If he met his killer there then his car had to be nearby, but you haven't found it.'

Sam shook his head.

'Doesn't that mean that his killer must have taken him there, either dead or alive?'

'We're checking the lay-by for tyre tracks, but so many vehicles park there, including our own ones today. I'm not holding out much hope of finding anything.'

'I think I saw him yesterday,' Loveday said.

Sam's head jerked up. 'You saw Walter Allen? Where?'

Loveday put up a hand. 'I'm not certain, but it looked like him. Walking along Boscawen Street. I thought he might be on his way to the museum.'

'It can't have been him. His wife says she waved him off to London early yesterday.'

'He could have gone via Truro. I suppose it's possible to drive all the way to London and back in the same day,' Loveday said. She looked up and met Sam's eyes. 'Or his snooty wife lied to you.'

That thought had crossed Sam's mind as well, but why would she? And then he remembered the cases all packed in the hall and ready to go . . . but go where? She'd said London. They needed to check with her publishing company, and Walter's tailor in Savile Row.

He was still thinking about that when Loveday said, 'I have some good news for you.' She put the wine glass she was holding on the low coffee table and sat down.

Sam looked up. 'I could do with some good news right now.'

'We've ditched the ancient relics feature.'

He put his glass down beside Loveday's and stared at her. 'Really?'

She nodded. 'Merrick felt it was too sensitive given everything that's been going on — and I agree with him.'

'And so do I,' Sam said, sinking back in his chair. 'You've no idea how pleased I am to hear that.'

'The idea hasn't been cancelled; we'll still be looking at it some time in the future. I want to research Carn Hendra and the old fogou and build an article around that. I just won't be doing it right now.'

'Sounds like a good plan. I'll even help you once you get down to it.'

'I may keep you to that.' Loveday smiled.

She waited until she thought Sam was relaxed enough before suggesting a stroll along the beach. The tide was out and the moon had transformed Mounts Bay into sheets of silver.

Loveday took Sam's arm and put her head on his shoulder as they walked towards the Marazion Marshes. It was a popular bird reserve and at this time of year visitors were often lucky enough to catch a glimpse of nesting herons.

'I've been thinking about Eva Penney,' she said. 'When will you know if it was her at that place out on the Lizard?'

'We're hoping to get DNA results tomorrow. Eva left a few things behind in her room at the pub. We can cross match them.'

'If it is her, she didn't end up in that barrow on George Pawley's land by coincidence. Whoever dumped her there knew about the site.'

The thought had been running round and round in Loveday's head all day. There was something at the back of her mind . . . something she couldn't quite remember. And the more she tried the further away it became.

'Have you ruled Tom Scobey out of the investigation?' she asked, and felt Sam's shoulder stiffen.

'You know I can't discuss that with you.'

'But it was me who told you who he really is.'

Sam stopped and turned her to him. A

breeze had got up and was rippling waves across the bay. 'You never did explain how you happened to know that . . . I mean what you and Maya were doing at his cottage.'

Loveday sighed. 'Poor Maya is still all over the place. The man she loved has been brutally murdered, Sam. She needs a friend and she trusts me.'

'What's that got to do with Tom Scobey, or should we be calling him William Bentley?'

'He's Bentley in London and Scobey down here. I think it's his business who he wants to be.'

'It's also my business, Loveday. This is a murder enquiry. Everything is my business.'

'You didn't mind dragging me into it when you wanted me to read that awful Desmond Height novel though.'

'You were helping me — and you did. You have to agree it was interesting seeing that room where Allen works.'

She nodded; there was no denying it. It was a fascinating place. She was picturing the big desk, the view from the window, the book-lined walls. She stopped, rooted to the spot.

'That's it,' she said. 'That's what I've been trying to remember. Walter Allen *has* written a book about Cornish antiquities. I saw it that day in his study. It was there in his bookshelves.'

'Well, we knew he was interested in the subject, he said so.'

'No, you're missing the point, Sam. If he wrote a book he must have done research. What if he discovered that burial chamber on farmer Pawley's land?'

# 24

Loveday parked by the pub, having decided to walk to Tom Scobey's place. She knew she shouldn't be poking her nose in but she had a feeling that the man was the missing link for all the terrible things that had happened.

As far as she could gather he had told Sam no more than he'd said to her and Maya. He was still maintaining that he'd only gone to London to check up on his flat. She didn't believe that any more than Sam had.

She had no idea what she wanted to say to the man, only that she had questions and a feeling that only he could give the answer.

He obviously wasn't the ageing penniless hippy he'd tried to present himself as. He was educated, he knew about art, and judging by what Maya told her she had caught sight of him typing into his computer one day, he could also write.

So what was he doing living like a tramp down here in Cornwall? It was his right to do that if he chose to of course, but why all the mystery?

She knew she shouldn't be approaching him. If he really did know something about the murders then it was Sam's job to find out, but then Maya had asked for her help.

There were two tracks through the woods to Scobey's cottage and she took the narrower more direct one. The path was strewn with broken twigs and she wished she hadn't decided to wear the open sandals. Her poor feet . . . they would be scratched to ribbons before she reached the cottage.

Loveday was still working out how to approach the man when the cottage came into view. She stopped, staring in annoyance as she recognized the car parked outside the property. It was DC Amanda Fox's green Mini. She hadn't known there was vehicle access to the place.

Well, that put paid to her plans for a cosy chat with Tom Scobey. She drew back into the trees, worried that Amanda would suddenly appear and find her here. She could imagine how much the woman would enjoy telling Sam that his girlfriend had been interfering in his case.

On the other hand, she hadn't come this far only to give up now.

She moved carefully through the trees, avoiding the path where she might be spotted, and slipped around the side of the cottage. That's when she saw the open window. The voices were distant. Loveday put her ear to the gap. She could just make out a woman's voice. It sounded harsh, angry — but it wasn't Amanda.

Confused, she pressed herself against the damp wall trying to catch the words.

'Police ... won't be missed ... shouldn't have interfered ... not so clever ... killer!'

Loveday put a hand to her temple. What was going on? She thought she recognized the voice, but it didn't make sense. Why was Amanda not speaking up? It wasn't like her.

Judging by how muffled the voice sounded she worked out that the people had to be in a room at the front of the house. Keeping close to the wall, she inched round the cottage. Loveday no longer cared that Amanda might discover her, something far more serious was going on here.

Both of the front windows appeared to be shut tight, but there was a tiny gap at the door. It hadn't been closed properly. Loveday moved forward and put her hand on it, praying it would not creak as it swung open. It didn't.

Her heart was in her mouth as she stepped into the dark, narrow hall.

'You really shouldn't poke your nose into other people's lives,' the woman was saying. 'And don't try to justify it by claiming it's your job.'

'Let her go, Milly.' It was Scobey's voice. 'This has nothing to do with her. She doesn't know anything.'

'Elizabeth, not Milly,' Elizabeth Callington snarled. 'Milly is dead.'

'OK, I'll call you Elizabeth if that's what you want. Just put the knife down.'

Loveday felt the blood drain from her face. Amanda might not be her favourite person but she didn't want her dead, and this woman was threatening her with a knife! But why? None of it made sense.

Her hand went to her jacket pocket where she could feel the bulge of her mobile phone. She had to get help, but it meant creeping back outside to where she wouldn't be overheard. Her heart sank when she glanced down at the phone and realized it was useless. She hadn't charged it the previous evening.

Loveday could feel the panic rising. She tried to remember the layout of the room from when she'd been in there with Maya and Scobey. It was the kitchen. She was picturing the bare stone floor, the old black range, the big scratched oak table, and some chairs. She remembered the door to a smaller adjoining room at the back of the cottage that Scobey had used as a study.

She listened. It sounded like that door was being thrown open now. She detected a dragging sound.

'You didn't have to knock her out.' Scobey's words were laboured, breathless. Loveday had a vision of him dragging

Amanda's lifeless body into the other room.

'And for God's sake put that knife away, Elizabeth. I'm going nowhere.'

She heard a door slam shut and then it all went quiet. What was going on? Were they still in the room? She didn't know. Perhaps there was another way out of the cottage? But from memory she recalled the only way to the back door was at the end of this passage — and they would have to pass her to reach it. She shuddered.

Elizabeth was speaking again. Loveday held her breath.

'I didn't recognize you at first.' She gave a little laugh. 'Well, you're not exactly the flash man about town you used to be.'

'I'm done with all that; I'm out of the rat race. This is my life now.'

'Some rat race,' Elizabeth scoffed. 'William Bentley was Harper and Harper's top dealer, their big noise in the city. You had all the trappings of wealth — the penthouse flat, the yacht, the cars — and you gave it all up to bury yourself in this

Godforsaken place. It doesn't make any sense.'

'I told you, it's what I wanted. You forget that I am now a celebrated author. You created me, Elizabeth. I am Desmond Height.'

Loveday frowned. What was he talking about? Walter Allen was Desmond Height. Wasn't he?

'I don't remember you raising any objections to ghost writing Walter's books, although I did wonder why you would want to.'

Elizabeth allowed her mind to drift back to the day two years earlier when Walter announced he had found a new great writer. His work had been getting worse with every book. He was burning out and it was showing in his sales. They had been on the lookout for a ghost writer for some time, but it had to be someone they could trust, someone they could convince would one day have a publishing contract in his own right, after he had successfully ghost written his first couple of Desmond Height books of course.

Elizabeth hadn't trusted Walter to find that person on his own. But fate had taken a hand and delivered Tom Scobey to them. She still hadn't been convinced when Walter said he'd been approached by an unknown writer and was sure that this was their man.

Her heart had given an alarming lurch when that man walked into Walter's study in Hillcrest. He'd given his name as Tom Scobey, but Elizabeth had been in no doubt who he really was. She shuddered now, remembering the moment again.

Walter had come forward. 'This is my wife,' he'd said.

Scobey had moved towards her, offering his hand.

She'd taken it with a condescending smile. Her hand had felt small and fragile in his. It had set her heart fluttering. Even now she had to steel herself against the emotions that had swept through her.

'My husband has shown me some of your work, Mr Scobey.' She had arched an eyebrow. 'Very impressive.'

Scobey's polite smile had widened. 'Coming from you that's praise indeed.'

She'd been about to thank him when Walter had cut in. 'Not that we think you are ready to go it alone you understand. You still have some way to go before you're ready to be launched on the world.'

The way he'd crossed the room and put an arm around the man's shoulders had irritated her.

'But we'll soon knock you into shape.' Walter had turned back to her. 'Won't we, darling?'

Elizabeth remembered flashing her husband a smile, allowing it to stray in Scobey's direction. 'We will,' she'd said.

She looked across the room at him now, in his pathetic old rundown cottage. 'What about you, William, when did you know I was Milly?'

'I didn't. Not for sure . . . not until I met Jamie.'

Another silence, and then Scobey said, 'Was it you, or Walter, who killed him?'

Every muscle in Loveday's body tensed. She hardly dared to breathe. The quietness on the other side of the door felt like it was stretching into eternity.

And then Elizabeth said, 'It was Walter. He killed Jamie.' The woman's tone had lost all its command. She sounded defeated.

'Don't pretend you cared about Jamie,' Scobey yelled at her. 'You sold our child. You sold Jamie for money to the Roscows. How could you do that?'

'How?' Elizabeth screamed back at him. 'Are you forgetting you dumped me, William? I was fourteen years old for God's sake. You seduced me and then you dumped me.

'Have you any idea how that felt? My folks were so far off their heads with drink and drugs most days that they hardly knew I existed.

'The children's home certainly didn't want me there. And the girl I shared a room with only wanted somebody to help her find punters around the London clubs.

'You were the only one who threw me a crumb of kindness. I trusted you, William, but you were just like all the others.'

Scobey groaned. 'It was a drunken one-night stand, Elizabeth. You told me you were eighteen. And if I remember correctly, it was you who seduced me.'

'You could have checked I was all right afterwards.' Her voice was trembling. 'But you were so keen to get me out of that swanky London pad of yours . . . '

Loveday could hear the catch in her voice.

'I was pregnant,' she cried. 'You left me with your child inside me, and you didn't care!'

'I didn't know you were pregnant. How could I? You never told me.' He released an exasperated sigh. 'Of course I know why now. You saw our child as a meal ticket! Why didn't you come to me? I would have made sure you were looked after.'

'But you wouldn't have married me,' she spat back. 'Would you, William?'

More silence. Loveday was trying to take stock of all these shocking revelations. Why was Amanda not chipping into this conversation? If they had put her into the smaller room she should be battering the door down by now. It wasn't like her to be so quiet. What had they done to her?

Elizabeth's voice was chilling again. 'I found the letters, William. I read them . . . all that slush you and Sarah Roscow wrote to each other. I was disgusted.'

'Those letters were private!'

'You believe you deserved your privacy . . . after the way you treated me? I don't think so. You needed to be punished. I thought about it for weeks after that. You needed to pay. I mean really pay.

'Ideas swam round and round in my head. I considered blackmail, but that was only money. I needed to do more than that.

'It was then that I discovered I was pregnant.

'I had checked up on your fancy piece. We weren't allowed to use the computer at the children's home, but I used to sneak into the office when the fat secretary woman wasn't there. Quite the socialite, your Mrs Roscow — and oh so sad that she and her banker husband couldn't have children.'

Loveday could hear the woman breathing. She must have been on the other side of the door.

'That's when it hit me. The plan was magnificent in its simplicity — a way to get even with both of you. I would sell my baby to the Roscows. I'd get lots of money, and neither you nor your lady friend would know the child she was bringing up was yours and mine, William. Conceived on your drunken night of shame with a child prostitute.'

She laughed. 'It was the ace I kept up my sleeve . . . the story I could take to the tabloids any time I wanted.

'You can't imagine how much pleasure that still gave me all these years later every time I sat across the dinner table from that bitch.'

'You truly are evil, Elizabeth.'

'No, killing Jamie . . . that was evil. You wouldn't have let Walter live either, not if you'd known he had killed our child.'

'There were other ways of taking revenge,' Scobey said.

'You mean by withdrawing your services as a cheap novelist? I don't think so. If the book-loving public were to discover that it was you writing those last two detective books and not Walter the sales would have plummeted.

'I wouldn't let you do that, William. I have investments tied up in those books.'

'And that's how I would have destroyed both of you,' Scobey said. 'I'm beyond caring about my reputation. The newspapers would have loved that William Bentley, the well-known recluse who was once a celebrated financial dealer in one of the biggest London banks, also ghost writes trashy detective novels and publishes them as Desmond Height.'

'You'd be ruined,' Elizabeth said.

'I'm already finished. You and Walter did that when you killed Jamie.'

'It was him . . . I told you. I had nothing to with Jamie's murder.'

'That doesn't even make sense, Elizabeth. Why would Walter want to kill Jamie? They were friends.'

'Jealousy. He discovered who Jamie really was.'

'I'm not buying that,' Scobey said. 'You'll have to do better than that.'

In the silence that followed, Loveday could feel her heart racing.

'Would you like to hear my version of events?' Scobey started. Elizabeth must have nodded, for he continued. 'Jamie was wary of Walter. He knew his parents had asked him to spy on him.

'I believe he discovered what happened to Eva Penney. She never went to Australia, did she, Elizabeth?'

'How did she manage to send a postcard from Sydney if she wasn't there?' Elizabeth's tone was sneering.

'We don't know she did send that card. What we do know, or at least what I believe, is that her body was found here in Cornwall.'

'She obviously came back then.'

'Or never left in the first place. This is what I think happened, Elizabeth.

'I've seen that postcard. It was behind the bar at the pub back then.'

'Well, there's your proof,' Elizabeth snapped.

But Scobey didn't sound convinced. 'I knew Eva, and she didn't strike me as the kind of girl who would take herself off to the other side of the world without a word. If she really had planned to move

345

to Australia, she would have been full of it.'

Elizabeth said nothing.

Scobey continued, 'so I checked up on what major events were going on in Sydney when that card was sent. And guess what I discovered?' He paused. 'A three-day international book festival — and you were there, Elizabeth. I've seen your picture online at an awards ceremony.

'It was you who sent that card, wasn't it?'

Silence.

'Did you kill Eva?'

'It was Walter,' Elizabeth snapped. 'I had nothing to do with it.'

'But you knew!'

'OK, so I knew,' she exploded. 'Stop badgering me. Walter was a wimp. He could barely wipe his own nose never mind dispose of a body. Is that what you wanted to hear? OK. I helped him get rid of the bitch.'

Scobey gave a loud sigh as though collecting his thoughts, and then said, 'Is this all about Walter and Eva having a fling?'

Elizabeth didn't answer.

'Fine, I can probably work it out by myself anyway. Walter grew tired of the girl — as he surely would have — Eva threatened to tell the world about their little secret.

'Walter panicked and killed her. But why bury her way out on the Lizard, and why in that place?'

There was a pause, and then Elizabeth said, 'Because he knew about the burial chamber.' She was sounding calmer. 'He was interested in all that stuff. He even wrote a book about it years ago that nobody bought. He remembered the place from his research.

'It wasn't a bad idea as it happened. He'd worked out that even if her bones were one day discovered, no one would be suspicious because she would be just another skeleton amongst so many others.'

Another pause. 'I believe Jamie somehow found out about this and confronted Walter with it . . . '

She left the sentence unfinished, but not before Loveday had heard the catch in her voice.

Loveday moved her weight from one foot to the other, trying not to groan at the cramp that had seized her left leg. She didn't see the front door slowly open behind her, or feel the hand coming up over her mouth to stifle her cry.

# 25

The hand was slowly withdrawn from her mouth. Loveday could feel the blood coursing through her. Was Elizabeth standing behind her with her knife? She slowly turned, hardly daring to breath.

Amanda! Her cheek was bruised and there was a cut above her eyebrow. She put a finger to her mouth, instructing Loveday to be silent. And then she pointed outside, beckoning for Loveday to follow.

They crept out of the cottage, keeping their heads well down as they passed the kitchen window and headed for the cover of the woods.

They didn't stop until they were sure they were out of sight. Loveday slumped against a tree, her heart still racing. 'God, Amanda,' she gasped. 'I thought you were dead. How did you manage to get away?'

'She didn't bind my hands as tightly as she thought when she got him to drag me into that back room. I managed to wriggle them free and untie my feet.

'The window wasn't exactly big. I'm still not sure how I managed to squeeze out without them hearing.'

Loveday and the ginger-haired detective might have their differences, but she'd never been happier to see anyone in her life.

'Did you hear any of what they were saying?' she asked.

Amanda nodded, but she was already on her phone, giving their location to the person at the other end, and issuing instructions to bring help.

She turned back to Loveday. 'I'm going back inside, but you stay out here till the others arrive. I need to see what else I can pick up.'

'You don't really think I would let you go back there on your own. You're hurt. If anybody is going back into that place it's going to be me.'

Amanda gave her a warning frown. 'Why can't you simply do what you're told for once? This is my job. Stop interfering and let me get on with it.'

But as she spoke she swayed and Loveday made a grab to steady her before she slumped against a tree.

'So you're fine are you? All we need is for you to collapse like that inside the cottage and where would we be?'

She tilted her head and studied her for a moment. 'I'm not trying to take over, Amanda. Really I'm not. But you're obviously not fit.'

She sighed. 'Look, you sit here on the grass for a bit and have a rest.'

'I'm fine,' the woman said crossly. 'I need to get back in there.'

'Give me your phone.' Loveday held out her hand. 'I'll record everything they say. And let's hope Elizabeth doesn't go looking for you in the meantime.'

Amanda closed her eyes as Loveday crept off. If she got herself killed it would be all her fault. How would she explain that one to Sam Kitto?'

Loveday had crept back inside the cottage and took up her old spot in the hall beside the kitchen door.

351

It was some time before anyone spoke, and then . . .

'How did you get Walter up to that stone circle without rousing his suspicions?' It was Scobey.

'I told him you had set the next book there . . . said we needed to get some atmosphere, take a few photographs.'

'And he fell for that?'

'Why wouldn't he?'

There was a chill in Scobey's laugh. 'There isn't one scrap of humanity in you, Elizabeth, is there?'

'I'm a survivor, William. You should know that. I'll kill you too if I have to, so don't you get too confident.'

'You mean that's still negotiable?'

'Depends on you, my darling. We can launch you into a wonderful new writing career and no one need ever know you wrote those terrible Desmond Height novels.'

Loveday glanced down at Amanda's phone to make sure it was still recording when, to her horror, it suddenly burst into life with a jarring ring. They'd

352

heard it! Already the door was being flung open.

Loveday glanced at the phone. It was Sam. In the split second before Elizabeth rounded on her, she hit answer and yelled, 'Scobey's cottage, Sam! Come now!'

She heard Sam call her name before the phone was snatched from her hand and dashed to the floor.

Elizabeth grabbed her by the throat. 'I don't like people snooping on me.'

Loveday hadn't seen the knife at first, but now she could feel the point of it at her neck.

Scobey was beside them. 'Let her go, Elizabeth. It's all over now.'

He went to the door of the back room and pushed it open and pointed to the tangle of rope on the floor.

'Your prisoner has escaped. The police know what's going on. I expect they will be here at any moment.

'If you want to escape you have to go now . . . run!' he shouted at her.

Loveday could see the woman's desperate eyes moving as she made a panic decision. 'We'll both run,' she said, pushing Loveday towards the door. 'You are my ticket out of here.'

A line of armed police emerged from the trees as they moved out of the cottage. Loveday gasped when she saw Sam stepping in front of them.

'Let her go, Ms Callington,' he said calmly. 'It's all over now. There's no need for anyone to get hurt.'

Elizabeth's eyes narrowed. 'Tell your people to back off, Inspector, or I'll kill your girlfriend.'

Loveday could feel the point of the knife prick into her back. The woman wasn't joking.

'Are you all right, Loveday?' Sam's voice was brittle.

'She's got a knife, Sam.'

'Move away, Inspector, and tell them to put their guns on the ground. We are going to use that car.' She nodded to Amanda's Mini. 'And I don't want to be followed. There's a gun in my pocket too, and it will be trained on your lady friend here.'

The armed officers lowered their

weapons as Elizabeth gave Loveday a push towards the car.

'Put the knife down, Elizabeth.' It was Scobey. 'I'll be your hostage.' He had taken a stride towards them, coming up on their left.

Elizabeth glanced across at him, and in that split second, Amanda sprang at them, snatching Loveday from the woman's grasp, and diving for safety.

Sam and the others surged forward and grabbed Elizabeth as the knife flew out of her hand and clattered to the ground.

It was over in seconds. Loveday caught her breath as she watched Elizabeth being led away.

'Sorry I had to be so rough. Are you OK?' Amanda said, not looking the slightest bit sorry. She had enjoyed it.

Loveday had landed with a thud, with Amanda on top of her. She was struggling to her feet, rubbing the hip she knew would be a mass of bruises by the morning. The detective had been a bit more enthusiastic than Loveday had considered necessary, but she had got her away from the mad woman with the knife, so she smiled. 'You did well, Amanda. I'm very grateful.'

The detective responded with a glance in Sam's direction. 'All in the day's work,' she said.

# 26

It was late when Sam got back to Marazion. He smiled when he saw the cottage lights were still on because it meant that Loveday had waited up for him. She came out to meet him when she heard his car.

'Is it really all over?' she said, stretching up to kiss him.

'It really is.' Sam sighed. 'There are a few loose ends still to tie up, but once Elizabeth started talking, there was no stopping her.'

They went into the kitchen arm in arm.

'So she's confessed to murdering Walter?' Loveday asked. 'What about Jamie?'

She followed Sam into the sitting room and watched him collapse into one of the armchairs as she waited for him to continue.

'She claims Walter killed Jamie because he was getting close to discovering the truth about Eva,' he said. 'Apparently Jamie had been suspicious about the barmaid taking herself off to Australia. Some of the locals had been muttering that it was so unlike her to just disappear. They said if she had really gone to Australia she would have been so excited that she would have been boring everybody to death about it for weeks before she left.

'He shared his suspicions with Walter and was going to contact the local plods.'

Loveday nodded. 'And Walter couldn't risk a police investigation?'

'That's what Elizabeth says, and we believe her. But they were both responsible for Eva's murder.'

'Poor Eva,' Loveday said. 'She didn't deserve that. How did she die?'

'Much the same way as Jamie, a blow to the back of the head.'

Loveday shuddered. 'I still don't understand how Elizabeth could sell a baby to the Roscows, and a few years later they didn't recognize her.'

'She's a clever, scheming woman,' Sam said. 'I think her getting pregnant by

Scobey was a cause for celebration for her. She didn't want the child, but she knew she could make money from it. She had read in magazines that Sarah Roscow was desperate for a child, but couldn't have one. It wasn't difficult to persuade her to agree to her plan.'

Sam was back in the interview room, reliving those hours of Elizabeth Callington's revelations. He said, 'The Roscows had a villa in Malta, and that's where they arranged for Elizabeth to stay until Jamie was born, although in those days she was still known as Milly Dunn, a homeless girl with drug addicts for parents.

'After the birth the Roscows paid her £10,000 for the baby, and Milly began to build a new life for herself. She stayed on in Malta and used the cash to change her appearance and take elocution lessons. She moved in with a rich older man who died and left her a villa and a lot of money in his will.

'By the time she came back to London and set herself up in the publishing business she was quite the wealthy lady. No one who knew her in the old days would have recognized her, which is exactly as she'd planned. She was Elizabeth Callington now. Little Milly Dunn was long dead.'

'I find that really sad,' Loveday said. 'It would be awful to go through life without having any real affection for anyone, not to mention love.'

'Her feelings for Tom Scobey, or should I say, William Bentley, were probably as close as she came to loving anyone,' Sam said. 'Although those feelings were so twisted up with revenge that I doubt if even she could recognize them.'

'Was she the one who left the note for Maya at the pub?'

'No, that was Walter. Elizabeth had already followed Scobey to London. He was a loose cannon and they believed he was about to let their big secret out of the bag.'

'You mean about him writing those dreadful Desmond Height novels?'

'Exactly,' Sam said. 'And they weren't about to risk that.'

'So what happens now?' Loveday asked.

'Elizabeth has been charged with the murders of Eva Penney and Walter Allen.'

'And what about Tom Scobey?'

'Well, he hasn't been exactly helpful to our investigation,' Sam said. 'He could have saved us a lot of wasted time if he'd come clean about who he really is in the first place.

'He is spending the night in one of our cells. I'll decide what to do about him in the morning.'

Loveday pursed her lips. 'He did offer himself as hostage in my place when the mad lady was threatening to stick a knife in my back,' she reminded him.

'And there's something else I need to tell you.'

★  ★  ★

They slept late next morning, only waking when they heard someone banging on the door. Loveday got up, pulling on her dressing gown and squinting at the clock as she went to see who was getting them up at nine on a Sunday morning.

'OK, OK, where's the fire?' she called,

pushing the tangle of dark hair out of her eyes.'

Two excited little people threw themselves at her as she opened the door.

'Auntie Loveday,' they squealed as she caught them. 'We've got presents for you and Sam.'

'Sorry.' Cassie grinned. 'Sophie and Leo couldn't wait to see you. 'Did they wake you?'

'It's fine.' Loveday laughed sleepily. 'I told them to let me know the minute you all got home. How was Disneyland?'

'I'll tell you when you and Sam come across for breakfast. Is half an hour OK?'

'Sounds perfect. Thanks, Cassie.'

Cassie's husband, Adam was stirring a huge pot of porridge when Loveday and Sam walked into the kitchen of the big house.

'You can't imagine how much we all missed this,' he said. 'There is a limit to how many plates of bacon and egg and fruit salad a person can eat for breakfast.'

Sophie and Leo rushed in when they heard the voices.

'The children are dying to give you

their gifts,' Cassie said, pulling a face. 'But just bear in mind that all this was their idea.'

'Gifts? For us?' Loveday clapped her hands.

'We chose them ourselves,' Sophie chanted, thrusting a large woolly donkey at each of them.

'I got you a tractor, Loveday,' Leo said a little more solemnly. 'And this is for you, Sam.'

Sam took the pink stick of rock as Loveday stifled a giggle.

'I can't think of any presents I could love more. Thank you both,' she said, holding her arms wide for them to rush in.

Sam cleared his throat. 'And that goes for me too. Thanks, kids.'

Adam began to dish up bowls of porridge, and the children ate hungrily.

Cassie had prepared a pan of scrambled eggs and had lined up a row of plates with toast.

Loveday began to pass the plates around. Following the events of the previous week she was enjoying the normality of it all.

After they had eaten, the children took off to watch one of the new videos they had brought back from Paris.

Cassie poured coffee for the four adults.

'So, what's been happening while we've been away? Did you catch your killer, Sam?'

'I apologize for my wife,' Adam said, throwing Cassie a scowl. 'She has no decorum.'

Sam laughed. 'It's fine. I'm sure Loveday will enjoy explaining it all to you, the main thing is that the case has now been closed and we had a successful conclusion.'

'Well, don't keep us all on tenterhooks,' Cassie said. 'What happened?'

Over the next half hour Loveday described the recent events, ending with the drama at Scobey's cottage.

'So you put yourself in the firing line again.' Cassie frowned.

Loveday was about to answer when Adam said, 'I still don't understand why you went to this Scobey's place. If you had suspicions shouldn't you have told Sam?'

Loveday shot Sam an embarrassed look. 'You weren't around, Sam. I did try to ring you.'

'You should still have waited,' Sam said patiently. 'I had already told Amanda to interview Scobey.'

'I didn't know that,' Loveday shot back.

'On the other hand,' Cassie cut in, jumping to her friend's defence. 'Loveday did get the evidence you needed to charge this Elizabeth woman.'

'And could have got herself killed in the process,' Sam said.

'I was never in any real danger, Sam, well apart from that knife in my back at the end.'

Cassie's eyes rolled to the ceiling.

Sam put up a hand. 'Don't ask,' he said, throwing Loveday an exasperated grin.

'What happens now?' Adam asked. 'Is the case all wound up?'

'More or less,' Sam said. 'I suspect a few more skeletons will come out of cupboards when it gets to court, and that's bound to mean some people getting hurt.' He was thinking of Charles Roscow. 'But hopefully it will give closure to Jamie's family.'

'And his friends,' Loveday added, thinking of Maya.

Cassie went to lift the coffee pot and put it on the table, telling everyone to help themselves to a refill.

'Now that the case is solved,' she said, 'can we get down to the really serious business?'

'And that is?' Sam asked, laughing.

'Loveday's inheritance, of course.'

Loveday grinned across at her. 'I've reached a decision about that.'

They all looked at her as she lifted her mug and took a sip of coffee.

'It was Maya's idea. I have to confess I wouldn't have thought of it.'

Sam raised an eyebrow. 'Go on.'

'I'm going to sell Carn Hendra to the archaeological society. Apparently they have been looking for a site like this to establish an interpretation centre. They might even rebuild the cottage as it originally was so visitors can see at first hand what a hard life people in Cornwall had to cope with.'

The idea was coming more and more alive as she spoke.

'The fogou is also there and could be included in the site,' she explained. 'They obviously won't be able to pay much for it, but that's not the point.

'It's about linking back to the past. This way it can be a kind of tribute to my family. I think Great-Aunt Martha would have liked that.'

Cassie was silent for a moment. It wasn't what she'd had in mind when she'd suggested Loveday should make the most of her great-aunt's gift, but the idea was growing on her.

Loveday glanced across to Sam. 'You're very quiet, Sam. Do you think it's a terrible idea?'

There was gentleness in his face as he reached across the table and took Loveday's hand.

Cassie and Adam smiled at each other.

Sam was gazing into Loveday's eyes. 'I think it's a wonderful idea,' he said.

# 27

'Am I under arrest?' Tom Scobey was facing Sam and Will across the table in the small green interview room.

The detectives exchanged a look. 'Do you think you should be?' Sam said.

Scobey grimaced. 'You could charge me with wasting police time.'

'I could. Maybe I should. You could certainly have been a lot more co-operative than you were.'

'I know. I'm sorry. I wasn't being intentionally obstructive. It was just that . . . ' Scobey's hands went up in a gesture of resignation. 'OK, so I had secrets. I wanted to bury them.' He looked away, a glint of tears in his eyes. 'And now I will be burying my son.'

'I'm very sorry,' Sam said. He glanced to Will, waiting until Scobey had composed himself before carrying on.

'How long have you known Jamie was your son?'

'From the first time we met I suppose. It was strange because I had no idea I had a child, but when I saw Jamie in the pub that day it was like looking at a mirror image of myself at that age. I was confused. I couldn't work out what was happening.

'He was Sarah and Charles' adopted son, that's what I'd read. But then I began to wonder if it was possible that Jamie could actually be Sarah's real son, hers and mine. I had convinced myself this was true and that she had told everyone she had adopted the boy so she would not have to admit to our affair. It made sense.'

He looked up, shaking his head. 'I was so angry. If I had a son I was entitled to know, but I couldn't bring myself to confront her. I couldn't bear to rake up the past. In the end it was Sarah who came to me.'

He met Sam's eyes. 'It was the day you brought her to Jamie's boat. She hadn't recognized me, not at first. But I went after her and told her there on the bank that I was William Bentley. I asked her to

369

meet me in Truro that night. She did. That's when she shared the circumstances of Jamie's adoption with me. I knew at once of course who Jamie's real mother was. I felt sick. It was all mixed up in my head. I had to get away. I have a place in London, so I went there.'

'I gather you're talking about Elizabeth Callington,' Will interrupted.

Scobey nodded. 'I had no idea who she really was at first, although she later said she'd recognized me at once, even though I was using a different name.'

'And her husband knew none of this?' Will asked.

'No, it was Elizabeth's little game. She enjoyed the subterfuge. She was a fantasist.'

Sam nodded to the young Constable in the room, who turned to lift the package leaning against the wall and bring it to them.

Sam untied the string and opened the brown wrapper. 'We recovered your paintings,' he said. 'It was Walter who broke into your cottage. Elizabeth had instructed him to check around and make sure there was nothing inside that could incriminate them. When he spotted the paintings he couldn't resist taking them.'

Scobey was shaking his head in disbelief. 'I can hardly believe all this.'

'We can't return them to you just yet because they are evidence,' Will explained. 'But we'll keep them safe for you.'

Scobey looked from one to the other. 'You're not locking me up?'

'No, you're free to go,' Sam said.

Scobey's shoulders sagged, and he hung his head. 'Makes no difference now. It's all over for me.'

'Maybe not quite over,' Sam said. The man looked up and stared at him with sad grey eyes. 'There's someone here to see you.'

He got up and opened the door for Scobey to leave the room, and then walked with him through the corridors to the front counter where Maya stood waiting.

Her face lit up when she saw him. She rushed forward, holding her arms out to Scobey. He looked confused.

'I've come to take you home,' she said,

glancing back to Sam and mouthing a 'thank you'.

Sam smiled and nodded back, reflecting on the news Loveday had given him the previous evening. Maya was having Jamie's baby. Tom Scobey was to have a grandchild.

He didn't know how all that would work out with Sarah Roscow and her husband Charles, but perhaps they had learned from their mistakes. Perhaps they all deserved a second chance.

Will came up to stand beside him as they watched the pair leave the station.

'Poor guy,' Will said, shaking his head. 'You can't help but feel sorry for him.'

Sam smiled. 'I have a feeling life is going to get a whole lot better for Mr Scobey.'

We do hope that you have enjoyed reading this large print book.

Did you know that all of our titles are available for purchase?

We publish a wide range of high quality large print books including:
**Romances, Mysteries, Classics
General Fiction
Non Fiction and Westerns**

Special interest titles available in large print are:
**The Little Oxford Dictionary
Music Book, Song Book
Hymn Book, Service Book**

Also available from us courtesy of Oxford University Press:
**Young Readers' Dictionary
(large print edition)
Young Readers' Thesaurus
(large print edition)**

For further information or a free brochure, please contact us at:
**Ulverscroft Large Print Books Ltd.,
The Green, Bradgate Road, Anstey,
Leicester, LE7 7FU, England.
Tel:** (00 44) **0116 236 4325
Fax:** (00 44) **0116 234 0205**

*Other titles in the*
*Linford Mystery Library:*

# BACKGROUND FOR MURDER

## Shelley Smith

In a psychiatric hospital, the head doctor lies dead — his skull smashed in with a brass poker. Private investigator Jacob Chaos is called in by Scotland Yard to investigate. But there are many people who might have wished harm upon Dr. Royd: the patients who resented his cruel treatment methods; the doctors who harboured jealousy of his position; even his own wife. With Dr. Helen Crawford as the Watson to his Holmes, Chaos must untangle the threads of the mystery . . .

# THE LIBRARY DETECTIVE RETURNS

## James Holding

Former Homicide cop Hal Johnson now works as 'library fuzz' — spending his days chasing down overdue books, stolen volumes, and owed fines. He doesn't miss life in the fast lane. But his police training and detective instincts still prove necessary in the bibliographic delinquency division. For such apparently innocuous peccadillos on the part of borrowers often set Hal on the trail towards uncovering greater crimes: fraud, theft, drug-smuggling, arson — and even murder . . .

# DEAD MAN'S PAIN

## Valerie Holmes

A man being pursued collides with Nicholas Penn. Assuming his pocket has been pilfered in the scuffle, Nicholas also gives chase. But the stranger fails to see a horse careering down the road, and is trampled by the animal, seemingly mortally. Later, though, Nicholas discovers that the man was no thief — and still lives. Mystified, he is determined to discover the truth behind the 'dead' man's pain . . .

# MORE SECRET FILES OF SHERLOCK HOLMES

## Gary Lovisi

Five untold tales of the great detective. In the first, Holmes chronicles to Watson a strange event at a freak show years before he met the good doctor. The second sees Watson throwing a birthday party for his friend — but danger lurks among the festivities. The detective and the doctor play golf at St. Andrews, and then are invited to Paris to solve a most perplexing art theft. Finally, Conan Doyle's Professor Challenger meets the duo, who arrive in the hope of preventing an attempt on his life.

# THE HUNTSMAN

## Gerald Verner

Superintendent Budd is faced with one of his toughest assignments in separating the strands of mystery that grip the village of Chalebury: a series of robberies perpetrated by the burglar known as Stocking-foot; sightings of the ghostly Huntsman; and the murders of a villager and a local police inspector. Interweaving with these is the suspicious behaviour of a frightened young woman who lives in a large dilapidated house with one elderly servant. Is there a connection between all these crimes and other oddities happening in the tiny village?